Two Deserts
Stories

Books by Julie Brickman

What Birds Can Only Whisper
Two Deserts: Stories

Two Deserts
Stories

Julie Brickman

Hopewell Publications

Published by Hopewell
Publications, LLC
PO Box 11, Titusville, NJ
08560-0011
(609) 818-1049

info@HopePubs.com
www.HopePubs.com

International Standard Book Number: 9781933435466
Library of Congress Control Number: 2013942842

First Edition
Printed in the United States of America

Grateful acknowledgement to the publications in which the
following stories first appeared: "The Cop, the Hooker & the
Ridealong" in the *North American Review*; "An Empty Quarter"
in *The Louisville Review*; "The Rainbow Range" in the *Barcelona
Review*; "Lust's End" in *Fireweed*; "Message from Ayshah" in
High Horse.

"The Night at the Souk" is the first chapter of
a novel in progress.

Back cover photo C Jeremy Horner/Corbis
Front cover, left photo C Patrick Lane/Blend Images/Corbis
Front cover, right photo C Pulse/Corbis

For my husband, Bob Hoyk,

love of my life.

1952 - 2012

Table of Contents

The Night at the Souk - 1

The Cop, the Hooker and the Ridealong - 13

Message from Ayshah - 48

The Dying Husbands Dinner Club - 55

An Empty Quarter - 73

Supermax - 89

Iggies - 110

An Old Arabian Folk Tale - 115

Gear of a Marriage - 126

Breakfast on the Balcony - 131

The Rainbow Range - 134

Lust's End - 148

The Back of Her - 157

The Lonely Priest - 161

The Night at the Souk

Within weeks, I realized it was impossible to get around this culture in Western garb, so I decided to take myself to the traditional souk and wander, maybe try on the local clothes: an abayah, a headscarf and a mask. It seemed simple, really. Wearing an abayah, I could explore this swathed, veiled country. I could discover ways through the maze of customs, innovate cutting edge tours to gratify our cutting edge customers. Maybe I could even make the love-you, hate-your-homeland romance work with Samir.

I'd settled into my responsibilities at the new branch of Gulf Travel, determined to develop programs to expand Western tourism, the only lucrative chunk of the travel industry the Al Rashid empire had been unable to draw and the reason I'd been hired as a partner in an Arab-run business in a country unfriendly to the West. Samir, the eldest son in the Al Rashid family and my collaborator in this precarious venture, was rabidly political. He oscillated between a teasing hostility and a prickly flirtation that was leading us, reluctantly, disturbingly, relentlessly, into a deep, unwanted involvement with each other. The clash between our visions spurred me regularly into excursions to forbidden areas of the city, my desire to penetrate its mysteries on my own superseded only by my desire to flaunt my mastery at Samir.

I flagged a cab with an Arabic rooftop sign. Local taxis were meterless, so I leaned into the front window to establish a price. The scarlet fez on the driver announced him as an immigrant Muslim, part of a huge labor force imported to do menial jobs, probably from Pakistan or some squalid, disease-ridden village in Africa, where a family of ten lived on his earnings. The dingy eyes below the fez jiggled with furious energy: twin maelstroms in a narrow, suffering face. Why bother to haggle, I thought to myself; if I saw his family, I'd probably *give* them my money. He shrugged off my butchered Arabic and signaled with a double flash of crooked fingers: twenty dirhams. Way too high for the short distances within the city limits. Suddenly I was into it. I splayed a hand and axed it with the other one: half the price. The speed of his agreement meant the ride would have cost an Arab five dirhams, tops.

Near the souk, the sidewalks jammed into a mass of turbaned, pantalooned, robed shapes, each on the move like rush hour Manhattan, except the pedestrians were all male and their pace was an amble. I pressed my face to the window and scoured the crowds for dark silhouettes to reassure myself that women did shop in the souk at night. Shopping might be too public a pleasure, an activity reserved for tarts and tourists. Not that the men would hassle me in any overt way. Islamic laws were strict, even in moderate countries. A man could be detained, clubbed, jailed, for pestering a woman in the street. All I had to do was shout, at least in the tourist areas, which were heavily patrolled by officers with blank, incomprehensible expressions that struck me as indifference or cruelty, but then most of the force was imported from countries where brutality had long been a government monopoly, like Syria or Iraq. The taxi inched through the thickening traffic.

Down a side street, a quartet of ebony shrouds swayed like shadows, blurring into the dusk. Like dominance, clarity belonged to the men. I asked the driver to stop, but he refused with a toss of his fezzed polelike head. Five minutes later, beyond a roundabout, he pulled into a taxi stand. Shoppers in limos, private cars, taxis, arrived and departed at a brisk pace, but in small groups, no one solo. It took a surprising amount of muster to overcome my fear and step alone into the crowd. I breathed deep like a yogi. Perfume and spice and sweat gusted into my nostrils, along with cigarette smoke, exhaust, and a whiff of pastry that buttered the air. Arabiana, Arabiana, I crooned, my nickname for this land when I loved it.

As twilight dwindled, the souk flared into a dazzling yellow incandescence; a brilliant desert light poured onto the wares like celestial polish, making them glow and sparkle with uncanny appeal. There was an overwhelming amount to see. Rows of shops clustered like teeth along the crooks of alleyways, each a jumble of wares: luggage, tee shirts, dishes, pots, cameras, perfumes, handbags, sandals, brassware, electronics, gold, jewels; you never knew what would be displayed with what. I moseyed through the crystalline light along streets narrow as trails and stared at wares in stalls, tents, vendor carts, shop windows, cataloguing what I wanted to buy: a couched camel of cured hide; a set of finger rings yoked by spidery gold strands to linked bracelets; an Aladdin-shaped oil lamp. Noise and vitality riffled the air along with racy scents and that crazy amber light. Whiffs of spicy perfumes and incenses mingled with oils crackling from rotating spits of *shawarmah*; nutty honeyed aromas floated from cafes and bakery shops. Black shrouded women hunched over counters and balance scales in gold shops, as they haggled for jewelry, the asset they could always claim as their own.

The winding, narrow alleys and crowded shops bewildered even my proficient sense of direction. Nothing was ordered or logical or familiar. The heaped wares were a challenge to appraise. Dress comprised a complex code for class and ethnicity, as impenetrable as the right cafe to enter. I could accidentally buy a piece of clothing that marked me as a servant or the wrong kind of Muslim.

The day I'd arrived in the country, my fluency in Arabic had suffered a staggering reversal. Entering the airport had been like stepping back millennia. People draped and robed in the wrapped fabrics of the East flowed around the terminal, as if time had warped back to the early days of Christianity when Jesus was still a desert prophet and a Jew. Pools of perfume and incense scented the air with powerful, mysterious fragrances. The diversity jazzed me into an aware sensuality, exquisite and pulsating. Yet it was the dissonance between modernity and antiquity that created the energy of the place, jarring and somehow inevitable, as if culture could be primal and evolved at the same time.

There stood Khalid.

Once my closest friend and colleagues at a travel agency in Manhattan, Khalid – Samir's father – was now CEO of the largest travel corporation in the entire Middle East. He had dressed in a dark western suit, like he used to in New York, but wore a *ghutrah* and *iqal* on his head, the white cloth and black headrope of the Gulf. I waved, my hand fluttering like my heart. He was already striding over, the white cloth flapping around features that could be carved in rock, the sleek trousers moving impeccably with his big frame.

He clasped my hand, placed his other at the center of his chest. The gesture was a primal one, an indication of the intention to live from the heart. I wanted to melt against him but held back, unclear what a hug might signify, and he mirrored me with a rock-still stance of his own. For a moment we hovered in that gap between cultures where no customs hold sway. On the far side of the baggage claim, a discreet distance behind their husband, the three co-wives who had been chattering on the plane, their uncovered hair as glossy as oil, their frocks as radiant as tropical flora, stood veiled and cloaked and mute. Watching them, the urge to share their language knotted deep inside me. Since then, my fluency had ebbed and flowed unpredictably.

A rack of *shaylahs* outside a market stall swung seductively in the jeweled light. *Abayahs* hung along the interior walls like paintings in a gallery. Abayahs had always struck me as too holy for public commerce, black robes of Islamic modesty to be sold only in homes and then only with the blessing of an Imam, like *halal* meat. It seemed sacrilegious to find them flaunted in the open souk, like seeing vestments of the clergy on display in a department store.

I glanced behind me. Women promenaded around as if they were free, yet *hijab* erased any sign of individuality. I couldn't see the expression on their faces or judge the attitudes in their bearings. I couldn't tell if they were young or old, flabby or toned, happy or sad. They were erased, blotted out, no bodies. I itched to tear open each abayah and see who lived inside. Their blackness affected my perception, afflicted me with cultural blindness. I felt obsessed by a desire to establish some connection with them, exchange a look, a moment, understand something of their lives from the inside. I needed to be able to talk about women's lives here; every Westerner would ask. Only women knew the secrets they lived by in this veiled land; only women could decode them for me, make it possible with Samir. I stole up to the display of abayahs and shaylahs, one thought in my mind.

I could see what it's like.

The shopkeeper spotted me fingering the cloth. *"Ahlan."*

The texture in my hands felt like thin wool.

"Come in," he invited, his undertone insistent.

It felt urgent to touch every headscarf, trace the scallops around their edges, examine the beadwork. Some were not completely black but rimmed by mosaic-like designs in metallic pinks and roses, indigoes and emeralds and peacock blues, or silver and gold leaf embroidery. Maybe I couldn't judge the implications of each weave and design, but I could find something.

"Try?" The shopkeeper swept his hands over his head in a draping motion.

It couldn't hurt. I crossed the threshold into the tiny shop.

A breeze as mild as puppy breath rustled through the dangling black shapes, making them sway like opera gowns. The perfumed silks emitted a sweet musty scent. The proprietor gave off a faint odor of olive oil and sweat.

He was a big, turbaned man, stooped, but with quick, skilled movements. "Try," he urged. His guttural 'r' sounded deep and full-throated.

He slipped an abayah from its hangar. The silk glistened like water in moonlight. Quaker gray pearls pebbled the stylish tucks along the shoulders.

"You are Muslim?" he said.

I buttoned the abayah right up to the neck. It fell into elegant Grecian folds. I twirled in front of the mirror, pleased with the look, as though by draping my form in black I had become enigmatic, ethereal. The shopkeeper waited for the answer to his question.

Two local men, first squat as a stump, the second fragile as a comma, marched into the store and began a voluble exchange. Pinned by the hot, yellow light and the wax and wane of their stares, I felt sure their banter was about me and grew awkward. The proprietor barked a call into the street and an assistant who looked about fourteen incarnated like a phantom. The boy arranged a selection of merchandise folded into cellophane bags in front of the stocky customer. Abayahs: the tree butt was selecting clothes for his wife. He jabbed his finger at one with such confidence in the ascendancy of his own taste, a jolt of insight rocked through me. How many wives had it taken to acquire that kind of assurance? He thrust the parcel into his cohort's hands while he drew out his billfold.

The proprietor plucked down a triangular headscarf and flapped it in front of my face. The plush fabric looked like a luxuriant version of the abayah's whispering silk. I placed it gingerly on my hair, wrapped it around my chin and tossed the ends over my shoulders as I'd watched the local woman do. My blonde hair vanished like a plane into a storm. Only the face was Western now.

The shoppers gaped.

I thought about what Maryam had said.

You should leave now, Emma. You are not welcome here.

And Ayshah.

You don't want those terrorist boys to catch you playing Muslim.

And Samir.

Politics here is a dangerous business.

"American?" the stocky man asked.

I knew I shouldn't answer. You never know who you're talking to. All four men seemed transfixed by the interchange. I gave a nod, Samir-like in its brevity.

"Why you want one of those?"

His companion's squirrely eyes slithered up and down the silk.

"Out of respect," I answered.

The aggressor hawked a glob of saliva around in his throat and spat a sound that would translate into something like argh. "Land is respect," he announced,

"Self-rule," and strutted out, his friend darting behind him.

The shopkeeper lost his few words of English and gushed Arabic in an attempt to explain away the unpleasantness. The poor man wobbled his turbaned head and mimed clownish faces at his customers' backs. His turban was frayed and gray with dirt, and under his arm the coarse cloth of his robe had torn. Afghani, I thought, there were so many here, poor and still countryless. His compassion and the extremity of his effort to make amends touched me.

I cupped my hands over my face, making a steeple at the forehead and sliding the thumbs over both cheeks. "*Burqah*," I said.

"No have." He draped a corner of the *shaylah* across my face like the veil of an old-time belly dancer and pulled it up to the eyes. In the mirror, I was blue eyes and white forehead. But still Emma, still recognizable.

The fabric was so dense it snuffed out the aromatic air of the souk, leaving only the hot gusts of my breath and the chemical smell of synthetic textile. Eventually, I could smell only myself, a decaying stuffy smell like the inside of a laundry bag. I clawed at the cloth on my face until the headscarf slipped into a circle around my shoulders and the hot yellow shopworn air rushed into my senses like a waft of fresh breeze.

After a couple of breaths, I pulled the scarf back over my hair and looked warily into the mirror. Nope. It wouldn't do. A mask was essential.

The traditional burqahs of Bedouin women resembled rigid Halloween masks or raven-black visors molded to the contours of the face. A splint down the nose fanned out into an oval, lip-shaped segment that covered or gagged the mouth, probably to protect it from sand. With a forefinger I tried to sketch one along the silhouette of my face. "*Burqah*," I repeated.

The proprietor unhooked a drab black cloth in the shape of a bandanna. It didn't look right but there were no alternatives in stock, not even the fancy burqahs with cats' eyes and gilded edges I'd seen in photographs. The double-layered bandanna unfolded into two identical squares, connected by a seam at the center, bleak and commonplace. How could I be transformed by sackcloth?

He snipped the basting thread at the seam. Making pyramids of his eyebrows, he begged pardon and permission for the transgression of assisting me.

His hands looked coarse and neglected, like dog driver hands, yet they trembled as he lifted the triangular black scarf off my shoulders. He doesn't feel safe, I thought. He bobbed the dull bandannas close to my eyes. They dangled from a funereal band about two inches wide. He pulled it tight as a headache around my forehead, trapping some stray hairs in the adhesive of the velcro when he fastened the two ends together in back. Two layers of black fabric blockaded me from eyebrows to chin.

The world bled of color, drained into shapes of gray like rainclouds in winter, like the grainy world of a silent movie, out-of-focus. The seam between the squares admitted a baton of sooty light, splitting the world into two shades of gray, charcoal and dove.

The shopkeeper flipped the outer cloth onto the crown of my head. The seam gaped open into a slit that bared my eyes and the sooty light flared into color.

The inner layer still concealed my face. I could see the world, but the world could no longer see me.

The proprietor selected a real *shaylah,* a wide oblong scarf, satiny to the touch, and draped it over my head, nodding approval as I tossed the ends over my shoulders. I vanished into black-specterdom except for two peering eyes. Which no one would dare meet for they knew not to whom or what household they belonged. The proprietor raved about how glorious I looked, how modest, how nourishing to the empty flask of a man's soul. A real woman of God, he declared.

I understood every word of his Arabic.

Now I could go where I wanted. I could speak to Samir in the tongue he brandished. I could get served by a pious merchant in a backlane cafe.

I haggled with the shopkeeper over cost. His first price was ridiculous, enough to feed a family of ten for a month. Though I was American, my income was substantially lower than the locals with their endless net of social entitlements dispensed by the tribal government as compensation for the absence of democracy. I countered dirt-cheap. The proprietor wagged his big turbaned head and humped his shoulders in a fatalistic way, as if such an offer were way under his costs, as if this particular outfit were handspun from imported tiffany silks, as if I had insulted his personal integrity and the *sharaf* of his family. His melodrama wasn't really a lie; he was including me in a game of barter as fundamental to the bazaar as hospitality to the desert, a ritual of camaraderie. I liked being an opponent, a genuine contender. With theatrical gestures, I started to remove the *shaylah*. This man owned a shop in the wealthiest trading city in the Arabian Peninsula. I swept an arm towards the handsome goods piled on the shelves: Look at all that. No way would I take the abayah at such a brigand's price.

In the end, when we settled on less than half his original very special low price for the American lady, a look of victory crossed his slouched face. "May Allah be with you and your children and your children's children." The pieties clicked from his tongue faster than barter as he smoothed my change in tattered bills I was sure he filched from a special drawer in his scored table desk. Behind the mask, I didn't have to restrain the impulse to make fat-chance grimaces when he told me piteously how he wouldn't be able to go home and face his wife or his brother until he chaffed up a better sale. It was clear he had come out on top of this deal.

I picked my way out of the shop, impeded by the robes tickling my ankles. I couldn't stride, only sashay in a truncated gait. The street pulsed with life, exotic yet familiar. No one froze stockstill at the sight of blond hair or uncovered flesh on a woman's legs. Men parted to make way; women passed so close their fabrics whooshed against mine. Surely this was my real arrival, this night at the souk when I donned an abayah and crossed into a border zone.

The Cop, the Hooker
and the Ridealong

At 7 a.m. Sunday morning, a police cruiser settles in front of our house. CIU is painted on the side in large blue letters and black vertical bars rib the back windows. I can make out the silhouette of a portly officer in the driver's seat, his neck swiveled to watch a house across the street.

My husband and I live on a quiet, residential street near the summit of a hill, far from the center of town. Broad and spacious in one direction, our road is cramped in the other, a harrowing drive around elbow turns where a micro moment of inattention could afflict or derange an existence. The back side of our house looks out on a canyon. We can stand at the window and gaze down at soaring birds, red-tailed hawks, crows, mockingbirds. In the distance, on a clear day, we can see the Pacific ocean, a deep teal color in yesterday's sun.

This is the second time I've seen a police cruiser parked here. Last time, they investigated the neighbor kitty corner across the street. Fred Wilson. Tall and thin and silver haired, Fred's a friendly man, always tinkering in his garage late into the night, the fluorescent lights glowing into the black pitch of the air. He and his wife used to spend the summers back east, in Connecticut people said, though I've never seen his wife. Zerine, next door, says she's a recluse, but someone else suggested she was ill. Because I saw a large woman go into the house one day last month, I imagine Fred's wife as obese, though in a cozy way, zaftig like an aunt from the old country who was comfortable in a vast, homey body, not possible here in California where fat is an indignity and aging rude.

Out back, a couple of deer are grazing on the brush, which almost makes me forget the sadness. At night, I roll pictures through my mind of all the beautiful sights and colors of each day. The deer, their tawny necks bent to feed, raise them still as steel, so I can see the flare of their moist black noses, arched and velvety at the end of tapered snouts. Their ears cock to gather vibrations, silent to me, and the round swell of their eyes look startled and soft, sorrowful I think. Some nights there are no pictures.

CIU stands for Criminal Investigation Unit I discover when I go out for the newspaper. On impulse, I walk over to the cruiser. A bloated, sweaty officer is taking notes on the computer screen mounted on the dash.

"Would you like a cup of coffee?" Awkward, I forget to say, in a little to-go cup, out here.

"No, ma'am," he says, twisting his sloping bulk in an attempt to shield the screen from what he assumes are snooping eyes.

"I just brewed some," I say, turning.

When he sees me start to leave without asking what's going on, he adds, "Just had a big cup. Thank you, though."

I realize, back in the kitchen, that he didn't just think I was prying. He thought I was inviting him in.

14

The Cop, the Hooker & the Ridealong

Years ago, when I was still a psychologist, I used to work with police, teach them things they didn't want to know about stress and human emotions. I rode in the patrol cars with them to find out what it was like. "Come on welfare night," they'd snigger. The night welfare checks were distributed was showtime on the streets, welfare and the full moon.

The first night I went out, a big burly cop tapped me for his car. Unusual: police don't like to have strangers in their cars, especially social science types, muddled by theory and too soft in the heart. But Max's partner was down with a flu, which later became pneumonia, and he wanted someone to work the radio in case of an emergency.

We cruised the downtown pedestrian mall where only black and whites and buses could drive. Pierced, tattooed, spiky-haired teenagers milled in front of glitzy shops, their music pouring into the crowds from loudspeakers and boomboxes. In the shadows, in recessed crannies where police eyes roamed long before mine, the shady deals went on. Folded into the darkness lurked the petty thieves, the pickpockets, the drug dealers, the methed-up, junked-down, ecstasied freaks on their fast descent into brutality, chicanery and death. In the incandescent brilliance of the station, Max introduced me to a haggard, sniveling woman, ashen behind the thick strokes of black eyeliner encircling bloodshot eyes. How old, he asked. I shrugged, thirty, maybe forty; who could tell. Eighteen, he said. Six months on the streets.

In the seedy part of town, where vagrants and drunks staggered through the streets and flophouses abounded,

Julie Brickman

Max drove me through hooker territory. They each have their corner, he explained, and they don't mooch on each other's turf. Beside the Italian pool hall and cappuccino bar, where I sometimes hung out by day, he pulled up next to a woman, shivering in a white fur jacket and stiletto boots.

"New meat on the street?"

She leaned into the car, nodded.

"Well, don't go down a block from here. You could get yourself hurt."

She wouldn't, thanks.

"There's some real nasty pimps hang out down there. Stay away from them." He looked her up and down, real slow. "You look like a nice girl. What d'you do by day?"

"I'm a nurse," she acknowledged, with an embarrassed laugh. "But I have a child, a daughter. You just can't get by on what nurses make."

He nodded, serious like. "Times are tough. You protected?"

"My mum was a hooker. She taught me the ropes."

"Well, good luck to you, sweet pea. And if you get in trouble, don't be afraid to call. The cops you see out here, they're after the johns. We got a new program going. But ask for me, Max. Ya got that?"

"Max," she said. "I'm Jeanne. J E A N N E."

Harlow, I thought. Because I associated cherry lips, wet with mystery, with harlot and figured it was brave to place one's future so near a concept that meant ruin.

We pulled away and I asked about the program. "Wuss whackers," he said. "We take their id, write down their names, ask if their wives know they're out here. Or their bosses. How would they like it if we published their names. Tell them we keep a list, for health reasons. List all the diseases they could get. Describe how their balls'll rot. By the time we're done, they're most of 'em are just glad to go home."

"Do you arrest any of them?"

"Nah."

I can hear my husband creep around the house, his hands squealing along on the two banisters we've installed, as he steers himself down the stairs. It's been almost three years since the first symptom of his disease appeared, an inability to run on the mini-trampoline. Six months after that, he said, "There's something weird going on."

It was early in the morning on a Sunday like this one. I was lolling in bed, luxuriating in the topaz light jewelling the canyon, in the sight of him lissome as the mountain lion he always looked for when we hiked. Now there was a bewildered look in his pond blue eyes. "My left leg won't do what my brain tells it."

Outside, the sea is grey today, the sky pale. The fishing boat is gone; in its place is the triangular white sail of a yacht, bobbing cheerfully on the small waves. Every night at dusk, a fishing boat chugs across the cove and, as the sun falls, a luminous spotlight shines from its side, as if a full moon has dropped right onto the deck to beam a path across the sea. A giant omniscient eye of light glows across the water and dispenses safety to that dark dark harbor. Shrimping, my husband explained, who had fished for a year up in the north part of the state. In bed,

I hold fast to that image of a beacon in the dark, let the roll of the dream-sea soothe me, until I drop at last into the tomb of sleep.

I suspect Fred Wilson is a batterer. It's the only reason I can conjure for the police to visit his house so regularly. Fred is too charming, I reflect, and his friendliness acquires an undercurrent of brooding anger. There is a story there, I feel sure. His wife hides in the house to staunch his jealous rages. He hoards all the money, dribbles Georges and Abes, a few Andies, out for groceries; come to think of it, I never see her shop. Or drive; both cars belong to him. Nor does she walk, though everyone around here walks. The streets are hilly, steep, great for aerobics; the weather is always mild; even the men walk, pumping small weights in their going-to-flab arms, breathing in heavy puffs like they're toning up for a marathon. Even when Zerine had a party for the neighbors, Fred came alone. I wonder if his wife is broken. Bruised on her face, or god help her, in her soul, like Jeanne would be now, if she'd made the wrong decision in the conundrum she faced when last I saw her.

Every time we rode together, Max took me to see Jeanne. Always she was standing there, on the corner beside the coffee bar and pool hall, tall and shivering in her fox fur, her hair piled in a brazen display of loops and curls, totemic in stature and pizzazz. Her skirts were short, her boots tall, and whenever she spotted us she strode over to the car.

"How's it goin'?"

"Got my girl in the Fraser," she said, shy-proud like a runaway who made it through her first day back at school. "*My* girl in the Fraser."

Max let out a hoot so prolonged it turned into a howl. "I'd better put my old lady on the streets," he joshed. "You're doin' well, girl. Watch yer back."

The Fraser, he groused when we pulled away. The fuckin' Fraser. He was happy for her all the same.

The disobedient foot seemed to be benign, Shane's primary care physician announced, but just to be sure he sent Shane to a neurologist, a specialist in Parkinson's. Parkinson's: all Shane's life he's dreaded the disease. His father had it, and once he tumbled on the steps of the Botanical Gardens and Shane, fourteen and immobilized, let him struggle to his feet on his own. A year ago, Shane's older brother, a rancher in Wyoming, had developed it. The look on Shane's face when he told me! Long and slack and inutterably sad. But nowhere near as unsettling as the look he gets now: the well of vulnerability in the half-open eyes, the drooping curve of his no longer mobile mouth, the sad downward slope of his thin shoulders, the flash of fear and sharpened awareness. I want to take him in my arms and rock him, but his balance is so chancy, I could tip him into a fall. Rocking has become too violent a movement. "You've got The Look," I say.

The Parkinson's doctor diagnosed neuropathy, and Shane came away reassured. He could do physical therapy or not; it wouldn't make the neuropathy disappear faster, though it might strengthen the foot.

Art is supposed to transform tragedy, but I have come to guess it's the other way around. Tragedy transforms art.

I get a peek into Fred Wilson's garage one day when he's on a tinker. Stacked against the far wall, impossible to see when both cars are tucked safely in their slots, is canvas after canvas of stunning acrylics. Three of them are facing outward, the most recent in the thick stacks of ten, maybe twelve paintings. I fetch the binoculars I use to watch wildlife in the canyon and train them on the pictures.

We live in a town of artists, profuse with galleries, festivals, and a summer pageant of *tableaux vivants* in which people are costumed and posed as famous sculptures and paintings each night. In our neighborhood, Zerine paints in brash sweeping watercolors and down the street Elaine Frick weaves textured wall hangings. The couple who rent have a life-sized figure standing on his hands poised in their window; in his bright blue coveralls, he looks zany in the daylight, apocalyptic at night. There is nothing extraordinary about paintings in a garage. I catch a glimpse of monochromes on aqua and green, tangerines and golds, liquid as emotion.

Fred closes the garage door, and its mechanical whir floats across the street to where I'm standing in our sunken patio, straining this way and that to try to find a decent angle. Eye level from the pit where I'm craning, our garden blazes into a palette of wild colors, chaotic and disorderly and insanely beautiful. Behind the pad-locked iron gate to his yard, Fred Wilson's plants are ordered neatly into lines of pots, ending with a wheelbar-row of red geraniums. The faded brown shingles on his house are soft with rot.

Fred walks across the street. "Livia?"

I let the binoculars slide onto the slate and walk out to the mailbox.

"How's the work going," he asks. Our house lay somewhere between fixer-upper and total-teardown when we bought it, the balconies so decayed you could put your foot through the planks, and we've been remodeling since the day we moved.

"Great," I say, though we're going to have to sell it, it has too many steps. "We're almost finished the exterior."

"Those balconies look larger than the ones you had before. You get a permit?"

"They're the same, exactly."

His nod is sympathetic. "That Design board's a bear, I hear. Backed up over a year just to get window permits. Tom, down the street, they turned him down, you know; he's been fighting with them ever since. He'll never get a thing done. They can make it so you can't stay in this town." He gives me a warm smile. Strands of his silvery hair, ruffled by the breeze, drop across his eyes, shadowing a frown onto his brow, which he shakes off with the abrupt upward movement that means *no* in some countries and *don't mess with me* in others.

In the summer, Shane and I traveled up to the north coast of Oregon to meet his brother and family for a weekend. Shane's brother, Earl, trudged slowly down the beach, his motionless right arm thrust into the pocket of his jeans. Shane slowed down to walk with him in the quiet way he would when we hiked together. "It gives me the chance to look," he'd say, strolling behind me, gazing at every vista, explaining to his New Jersey girl the California plants, the saucy yellow monkey flowers, the twisted branches of manzanitas, and the tree-tall spires of the yucca whose time to flower is right before it dies. I can see him now, beside his brother, two six-foot figures, one thin and lanky, blond hair feathering in the breeze, the other thick and sturdy, black billed cap covering his thatch of deer-brown hair. Their talk looked intense, but I know Shane was doing most of the listening. He probably drew up a list of questions to ask his brother before we even started on the journey.

Shane walks up and down the hall, the Parkinson's doctor watching him. The onset of weakness in his hand has escalated concern; you don't get two neuropathies unless the brain or the spinal cord is involved. Shane's left leg swings in a little arc with each step, lending a slight jerky motion to his gait. The doctor shakes his head. "It's not Parkinson's," he says. "Definitely not Parkinson's." I ask how he can tell.

"The Parkinson's gait is stiff, not plastic like this one. Small, rigid steps. Usually a shortened arm swing too, if there's any swing at all."

"And Shane's gait?"

"Spastic," he says. "The muscles aren't following through. They stop partway, pull back, instigate that little jerking motion." He points towards Shane's foot. The front is sloped towards the floor, as if gravity is exerting more force on the toe than the heel. Smooth and bantam, the arc reminds me of the undulating motion of a pendulum.

"You need a neuromuscular specialist," the doctor says.

The police cruiser is parked in front of our house again. It is late in the evening. Vestiges of salmon-colored twilight smear the charcoaling summer sky. The men in the cruiser dally for a while, conferring I assume, though it takes a very long time.

Once when Max and I went to answer a domestic, he pounded on the door then leapt aside, shouting, "Police. Open up." When I didn't follow suit, he grabbed my arm and yanked me over beside him. "It's a domestic," he hissed. "You never stand in front of the door in case they answer with a gun." The two cops ply open the front gate and bound to Fred's front door, where they scatter, one to each side.

Fred's house is obscured by layers of fence and garden. Darkness consumes the threshold, and the two officers and the wash of yellow light are quickly swallowed behind the thick, closed door. The cantaloupe streaks in the sky have dimmed and faraway streetlights are visible in the coal of night. I can see headlights moving along the Coast Highway, but, unlike the lantern eye in the harbor, they don't look friendly; they look lost and unsteady, weaving down a road far from home, popping in and out of view. Cold has descended with the dark, and a shivery feeling races across my skin.

The shivery feeling reminds me of the day Jeanne called my office.

"I *have* to see you," she announced. "Right away."

It took a while to find out who was calling, but when I did I said to come right over.

"Tonight," she replied. "Before my shift." She meant street, not nursing, shift. She meant after her daughter had been tucked safely into her expensive bed and an elderly babysitter had been installed in the living room, but before she hit the streets.

I was used to this kind of call. I got a lot of referrals from police, sexual assault centers, agencies that took in street kids. For reasons I never could identify, I'd gotten a reputation that I could be trusted. I think it was simply because I didn't equate bad luck or bad judgment with bad character, didn't confuse the result with the cause. Back then, to understand women's lives was radical; it gave me a reputation for being a tough babe, a feminist when to be a feminist meant something strong and edgy.

Plus I let people lie. I understood that the truth was too diminishing to bear except in glimpses, that they needed to make fictions from their experience just to get to sleep at night and back up in the morning. Storying, they called it, when they invented dreams about circumstances other than their own. Once they'd harvested enough resources to put the truth – ugly in spite of all the artistic claims about it – in a landscape vast enough to make it small, they would tell it. Truth had to be cut down to size or it would assault you again.

Jeanne came in at 9:30, a half hour later than we'd agreed. She was wearing jeans, tattered at the knee, and a ribbed black tee shirt. Her dusty hair was clipped short around her face, which made me realize the heap of black curls was a wig. Without the heavy makeup, her lips looked meaty but not as wide as I remembered, and the ginger of her eyes faded into her face, lightly spattered with freckles and shaped like a spade. Her lashes were short, her pale eyebrows plucked into inverted vees as though permanently lifted in shock. Her buttocks barely grazed the rim of the chair and she hunched forward, hands splayed on her thighs, so her weight rested mainly on her tensed legs. Undecided she was, in spite of the urgency of her call.

The chairs in my office were soft brown leather armchairs, vaguely Scandinavian in design. A marble side table, shaped like a half moon, rested flush against the wall; the tiny lamp on top emitted low light. I kept the therapy chairs angled slightly toward the windows, so my visitors could look out or at me, as they chose. Jeanne opted to seize my attention with her eyes before she started.

"I'm really fine," she said. "I don't know why I called you."

"It's always hard to figure that out."

"Really? Other people don't know?"

"If they do, they're usually just making something up."

"Lying?" She made the word sound casual, musical, though her torso tensed.

"Motivating themselves. Giving themselves a reason to get here."

She sat back a little. "I can make a hundred thousand dollars," she said. "For a few hours of mega work. Maybe ten grand an hour."

"Oh?"

"Bet that's more than you make."

I laughed. "For sure, I don't make that in an hour."

"In a month?"

"No. Not in a year."

She snuggled back in her chair. She had something I didn't and it made being here bearable. Relaxed, she began to cry. At first it was just moisture running from her eyes and her open mouth and nostrils, but then it seemed to gather steam, because it escalated into a gasping wail, and all her body went into participating, her heaving shoulders and abdomen, her jiggling shaking anxious legs.

It was not the kind of sob that needed Kleenex; the very act of handing her a tissue would inhibit the flow, so I sat and looked out the window, trying to give her the quiet acceptance she needed. The night was tar dark, and a watery light fell from the street lamp, making everything in its corona look blurry. I realized then that it was raining, a daily event in this northwestern city of tall boreal trees and profuse flora. It had been misty all day, the sky leaking a dampness that clung to the skin in a clammy film, but now a light rain slanted outside the window, one of those spacious rains in which every drop glides slowly along its own trajectory, mirroring for brief seconds the entire world on tiny rotating cylinders, reflecting birch bark and spruce boles and pine needles, the bright light of a window, the bowing fronds of a willow, a floppy-brimmed hat, the glint of a lost trinket, all of which seemed to be sliding and falling, as though the raindrops were motionless and the world topsy turvy, and suddenly I saw the two of us, Jeanne and me, in brown leather chairs, toppling and somersaulting, the lamp and the half-moon of the marble table tumbling with us, all strangely stuck in precise arrangement to each other while we rotated and swirled, and I turned back to look at Jeanne whose sobs were subsiding.

"Mwaah mwah fyah mwaaah." She looked up at me as though she were saying words, so I nodded.

Her eyes closed again and when she opened them, she gave her head a shake, stretched her arms in front of her, and said. "Can't believe I fell asleep like that. How much time do we have?"

"Enough," I replied, though we were already running over. First sessions often flitted around the fiery center of a problem. I reeled my mind backwards through the rain to retrieve what she'd been saying before she'd started to cry and realized it was money. The hundred grand.

"I was twelve," she said, "when my mom first introduced me to the life. I was early to develop, had my period for two years already. I felt, like, crazed with this Colossal Lust. Everywhere, suddenly, all I saw was boys. I couldn't think, I couldn't talk, I could barely see. But every night, I had my chance. Down would go my hands, rubbing, cuddling, fingering, until I found everywhere that felt good, the sweet satiny place behind and the little bud in front. Five, six times a night, and still it wasn't enough. I was at a Catholic school, you know, 'cause my mom knew. She'd been the same, and she said it would never go away. It was a talent, sex, the same as being gifted in athletics, and it needed mega attention. I was fourth generation, she told me, proud as all getout; my great great whatever grandmother had been a good time girl in the Yukon gold rush. She promised to oversee my training when I was old enough, and she did."

"How was that?" I asked.

"She started me off herself. She stripped me naked and stood me in front of a mirror, showing me all my parts, front and back, using a hand mirror to let me see everything between my legs. Then she took me to bed and taught me every sexy part of my anatomy."

"And?"

"Then she brought in men. Small ones at first, not the guys, but the pricks."

I smiled at the explanation. Not that she needed encouragement. This was a story she wanted to tell.

She seemed to relish every detail. The first man had been Pierre, a French Canadian. In her mother's day, the French had been renown as lovers, and Pierre was skilled but small; perfect to start with. That moment of entry! Never had she known such sweetness! But that was not what her mother had in mind by training. Once she had learned the ecstasy part of the trade, the love of pleasure that kept a whore at the top of the game, her mother taught her the skills, like how to clean up a man before you touched him or roll on a condom without his missing a beat; how to use your tongue to craze him or deep throat him or take him round the world.

Jeanne's face had a look of bliss that made me wonder what Eve had really known, and I sensed her reluctance to move on. "So what's troubling you?" I asked.

She bucked in her seat and glanced down at her watch. "Omigod," she cried. "Gotta go. I've got a regular, twenty minutes ago." She looked up at me and gave me a sly, sexy smile, cunning as a ray of sun as it fanned from behind a storm cloud. "You're just like me. You get a client going and they don't want to leave."

The spell of the session lingered between us, even as I explained confidentiality rules and where they ended: threats of violence to herself or others. Rising to leave, she cocked her head at me and cooed in her girlish voice of memory, "God, I feel better," and we set another time.

People think you get stories when you do psychotherapy but you don't. No one ever tells you about the floral bedspread that lay lightly over them as they listened to the summer crickets, or how they laughed on the Ferris wheel when they discovered they weren't scared at the top. I never found out anything about Jeanne's second profession, not how many tricks she turned in a week, nor what she actually did with them, nor whether women made offers. She worked three nights, short shifts, and the money was all hers; she didn't have an old man, aka a pimp, which was why she'd chosen a peripheral corner. I did find out, when we talked about fees – she always paid cash and never wanted a receipt – that she also had a sliding scale. And when it became relevant, she confided that the best relationship of her life had been with her mother, in a bungalow full of laughter and kindness on the endowment properties out on the peninsula. Her mother had died of Hodgkin's lymphoma, thirty-seven years, four months, and three days into her life, six months before Jeanne finished nursing college, eleven months before she gave birth to her own daughter.

Whenever anyone talks about assisted suicide as an act of mercy, they say, *But what if you get Lou Gehrig's disease?* While Shane was still certain he had atypical Parkinson's, I was madly reading about other neurological conditions that started with a dropped foot and progressed laterally to weakness in the hand.

The second entry on the Mayo Clinic website was Amyotrophic Lateral Sclerosis. The signs could be subtle, the doctors wrote, like "difficulty lifting the front part of your foot (footdrop)" or a weak, clumsy hand. Typically, the disease began in the limbs and then spread as weakness to all parts of the body, eventually affecting chewing, swallowing, speaking, breathing, and ending in general paralysis of all voluntary systems. Death usually occurred three to five years after symptom onset. That night, I slept on the pullout sofa so I could toss and weep in fear. In our bedroom, Shane, still innocent (could I keep him that way?), slumbered in his illusions, perhaps dream-building the plan for world peace he yearned to generate, perhaps dream-visiting the island off the coast of Turkey where he'd taught rebellious French children in an experimental school. Was it possible my next years were going to be spent, not going to Norway to study an evolved culture or to Israel to hesitantly explore my roots, but watching the person I loved most in the universe go through cruel agonies? Be robbed of every function while his crystal mind understood every step? Yet even then, my imagination failed to generate the horror of it, which lay in its very dailyness, the relentless decimation of every human power. There is no adjusting to ALS. It changes everything, nerve by nerve, day by day. A Biblical word suits it. Affliction.

Monday morning, I called the Parkinson's doctor and left a message. "Tell me, I said, "how did you eliminate ALS?" Neither the doctor nor his nurse called me back.

At the harbor, my husband and I spy an odd little bird, strutting along on thin orange stilts. His little gams take him faster than the three-foot-plus shanks of my spastic husband. Shaped like a heron, the bird has the rickety gait of a sandpiper and the long pointed beak of a fishing bird. His small but not insubstantial body is a mottled buff and brown, and iridescent tufts plume his crown and striate his stubby neck. On little spindles, he goose steps over to the side of the pier, making my husband and me laugh out loud at the silliness of his stride. Dockside, he peeks over the edge and then draws himself erect to elongate his neck. Stretch, stretch, stretch, he extends his wattled neck until it looks as long and graceful as the curve of a swan or even a great blue heron, which turns out to be his relative. And then this American bittern, this solitary creature of the coastal bays and marshes, steps delicately onto a mooring rope and tilts the rondure of his neck all the way to the water, closing his beak over something which we can only see as he steps backwards to safety, a silvery minnow curled in his mouth. Fluffing his feathers, he tosses off droplets and struts forth to another mooring rope to repeat the process. Cloud Chaser asserts the name on the prow of the yacht and I glance up to see the gossamer shapes of my favorite fantasies scud out to sea.

Max and I are out again, his partner's pneumonia having taken a turn for the worse. Just as we head towards Jeanne's corner, an urgent call comes in from the dispatcher. By now, I have run training sessions for dispatchers and complaint-takers, know they assess danger on several scales at once, including threats to life, risk to personnel, and crimes currently in progress. This one involves a belligerent drunk in a crime-infested hotel; it's hard to assess the danger level but so far it's victimless.

Max whips down a side street away from Jeanne's post and flicks on the lights and the siren. It surprises me how few drivers pull over, even when we zoom right up their tails, red and blue lights atwirl in their rear view mirrors. The sirens, I understand, can't be heard over the blare of music and talk radio. Max loops around a Toyota and a surprised Asian face looks out the window.

In front of a dingy red brick building, Max double parks and hands me the mobile radio. "Call if you think I'm in trouble," he orders, motioning me to follow him. Not another patrol car is in sight, though if it were a robbery in progress, Max would sit tight until at least one or more backups converged on the scene.

The halls are dim and grimy, too narrow for two people to pass without brushing.

The stench of boiled vegetables and human excrement mingles in the damp, suffocating air. The smell of piss could be booze, it occurs to me, as I inhale the pungent smokiness of tobacco or marijuana and try not to wheeze or choke. Max strides forward, not bothering to assess the sounds bleeding through the doors, voices underscored with music that might be TV sets left to play or arguments in progress. It is after one a.m.

On the second floor of the walkup is the flat we are looking for. Max pounds on the door and shouts, but doesn't wait long before he places his big meaty hand on the knob. It is unlocked and he goes right in, keeping his gun holstered, though I know he is mentally prepared to draw it in a flash. In the corner of the room, an old man, surrounded by pools of vomit, groans and shivers in a rocking chair.

"Hey, buddy." Max kneels next to him. "You ok, there?"

The old man moans and starts to gag, and Max leans away from the potential trajectory. When the puking sounds stop, he wraps his arms around the bony quivering torso and pulls the limp body into his own bulky frame. "Okay, buddy, let's get you to a hospital. You're too sick to stay here."

The old man is wearing a threadbare kimono that was a green and burgundy plaid before it faded. It is covered with wet patches of puke and body wastes that have slipped out his flaccid sphincter or slavered from some other failing muscles, and the odor of his unwashed flesh and clothing is sour and pungent. His unshaved whiskers grow white and patchy, and hair the color of wet rocks lies in a matted tangle against his skull. The veins at his temples throb like plucked guitar strings, and I feel sure they bong a drone into the ache of his brain.

Max wraps his big arms around the dying wino and half-drags, half-carries him to the door. "We'll take him ourselves, if the medics don't get here," he announces. Cued, I call in the request to dispatch, while Max bear hugs the grimy old thug and marches him to the street. No one in the building notices; used to it, I guess.

Outside, an ambulance is waiting, and I can hear the paramedics grumble how the ER staff will hate this one. They flop the old man onto a gurney and pull the straps too tight, making as if to hold clips to their noses.

Back in the patrol car, Max says, "Old meat on the street. Carve that in your brain."

I nod, though that wasn't what I learned. I learned that cops like Max go into places no one else will go and touch people no one else will touch. It made them mean and bitter or it gave them a compassion so deep they hid it away. And it never ever turned up in their war stories.

Fred Wilson catches me as I'm starting out on a ramble around the neighborhood slopes. "Zerine says your husband can hardly walk anymore. You need anything, honey, you be sure to call me." He matches his pace to mine.

I can feel the blade of his presence, just inside the margin of space I need to be comfortable and I angle my stride to get away. He steps into my space again, but this time it feels tranquilizing.

Fred's not a walker; he's a gardener and a putterer and a motorer, but he doesn't hike the local streets. His breathing is coming out in short puffs, and thin and elegant as he is, I wonder about the strength of his heart. His polished loafers clatter against the blacktop; not even shod in rubber soles, he didn't intend to go for a walk.

We walk along in silence, uneasy as choppy water. My mind races unpleasantly over things to say and objections to saying them as we pass the homes I know so well: Louey's dilapidated mansion rising from the nurtured blooms of her desert garden; the life-size stuffed jester of the renters cavorting upside down in the window; the cedar-tinted craftsman of Nosy Alice and Big Walt.

In front of the slope that's underpinned with steel girders strong enough to hold up a suspension bridge, Fred almost leaps in front of me, and I crash into him as he bids wait, stop, in a forbidding tone. The two of us teeter back and forth and it reminds me of the last time I walked with Shane. Shane was using a cane then, and I traipsed slowly alongside him, careful not to speak, for if I startled him, he could topple. When a car rumbled in the distance, I would zag to the center of the road to be sure, seeing me, they'd leave a wide margin. One day, as I was zigging back, our shoes brushed against each other, his to mine or mine to his, I don't remember. All I know is he teetered, teetered, teetered, and then plummeted full tilt to the ground. "Don't," he snapped, when I went to help him, as he hunkered in the brush near the curb, making plans for how he would get to his feet, gathering his courage to do so. It was the last time we walked the neighborhood together.

"Don't take another step," Fred warns, and creeps gingerly forward towards a cluster of rocks, where he bends over and peers at what appears to be a stick.

I go over, in spite of the hand he flaps behind him to warn me off, and the stick slithers towards us. I can see by its markings, it's a baby rattler.

"Watch it." Fred yanks me away from the curb. "They don't have the sense not to strike. And their venom is lethal."

He leaves his hand on my elbow, and I can feel the venom race through my imagination. I shudder him off and he removes his arm, as if stung.

"My wife was bit by one of those," he says.

I stare without meaning to. I'm wondering if he led her to it and ridiculing the thought at the same time. The baby rattler stretches its diamond-backed body, pale green like the branch of a sapling, down the steep side of the curb, and it reminds me of the bittern Shane and I saw, dipping his neck into the harbor. The rattler slithers gracefully across the street.

"What happened?" I ask, but Fred is looking around. "Kids," he says. "We can't let kids near it."

"Dogs either," I agree.

"I'll watch over it, and you warn anybody who's out."

I stride up and down the street, warning people. There aren't any kids, but several people are out with their dogs. Only one is off leash, and the rear of his thick body squirms as his tail thrashes out a happy rhythm. I grab his collar and the owner snaps the leash onto it, giving me a grateful smile. They both turn and I watch them wiggle waggle together up the slope.

"All clear," Fred calls. The rattler has climbed the other curb and disappeared into the chaparral.

Jeanne came for a half dozen more sessions, each one following roughly the same pattern. I learned a lot from those sessions, not the least to celebrate lust, starting with my own gentle hands.

Once Jeanne said that she'd discovered something her mother had never taught her.

"What was that," I asked, by now way too eager for her stories.

"I can hit the moon by fantasy alone."

"No," I said, knowing the challenge would provoke her.

"Absolutely. There's a secret to it." Her voice tailed off and hesitation suffused her face with a blend of defiance and wariness.

I looked at her, my expression serious and still.

"You're gonna laugh at me."

"Have I ever laughed at you?"

She laughed herself, a peal of joy. "I could do it right now, with you."

"Here we use words," I instructed, as much to myself as her.

"Meditation," she said. "You have to focus so hard you are your cunt."

I could feel myself imagining it. All of me became two soft upright curving lips, pink as oysters, perfumed as roses and mulch, and there in the center the well of life, tunneling to the core, the very essence of me. It wasn't hard to envision. As a therapist I believed most people thought with their genitals half the time.

"Ok," I said. "Then what."

"Then you add the action."

And there it was. The pulse; the very beat of life. The opening up to the world.

"You can do it!" Jeanne could see sensuality like I could see emotion.

"Probably," I said, drawing back.

"After that, you become the prick. The great swelling vulnerable sensitive sponge that you pretend is a club, a volcano, a gun, a torpedo."

I laughed. This is what you shared with your mother, I thought. Intimacy and joy.

She went on to describe how she mingled the two images into action, enabling herself to hit the moon anytime, anyplace. Later, she'd step back like a voyeur, examine it from a distance, invent whole scenarios she'd play out with clients, if they agreed to her prices. She could get up to a thousand dollars a trick for one of these, but it spoiled them as private fantasies, so she only sold them when they stopped enchanting her.

It was time to stop. Jeanne had mentioned money again, and I knew next time we'd circle back to the question that had brought her.

The appointment with the neuromuscular specialist was at a university medical center hospital, about a half hour ride from our house. An easy drive, the route took us along wide campus boulevards, where tall palms formed spiky mops of green against the sunny blue of the sky, past the university theater where we used to watch foreign films, when we still went out. The medical center was a large unassuming structure set back along a winding drive. Shane spotted the silvery coat of a coyote moving along a path in the dry grasses of a distant bluff.

It was early and the neurology waiting room was empty except for a man of about seventy who walked perfectly well. A nurse in beige scrubs beckoned Shane into a cubbyhole, where an inlaid platform scale, big enough to roll a wheelchair onto, let her chart his height, 6 feet, and weight, which had fallen to 152. At the rump of a crooked corridor, she installed us in a dingy, corner room. Angled like a hypotenuse across the center, the examining table looked exposed and vulnerable. The nurse guided Shane onto it, handed him a crumpled hospital gown, and left. Tiny orange guppies wriggled across the fabric, making Shane, swinging his thin bare legs against the side of the gurney, look frail and diminished. Chrome carts, unplugged machines, and rolling tray tables were stashed in corners, and the grimy mishmash reminded me of the old wino's lodgings, though for some reason what offended me was a vacant bookcase that sagged against wall.

Clipboard in hand, a neurology resident bustled in to take a history. "What was your first symptom?"

"A neuropathy in my left foot."

"When did you notice it?"

"Nine months ago, in January." Shane looked at me.

"No," I said. "The first symptom was earlier, last August, over a year ago. When you couldn't lift your feet on the rebounder."

We summarized all the developments through the Parkinson's doctor, the MRIs and CT scans, all of which had been forwarded. The resident tapped Shane's knee and ankle, looking for jumpy reflexes, and then slid a door key along the bottom of Shane's foot. Clinically, the response to this is a sure way to identify motor neuron disease, as are bilateral fasciculations or contractions of the tongue. Shane evidenced neither, though his reflexes were hyperactive, and he kicked the rookie neurologist several times. Clonus, the resident muttered, embarrassed that he'd forgotten to get out of the way. Shane's startle response was immense.

The senior neurologist was younger than I expected, in his thirties, with a pouchy, pockmarked face. He wore a dark suit as somber as his sad, hanging expression, and I found it all infinitely depressing. The ugliness denigrated the two of us and whole implicit trajectory of love, disease and death.

It was then I discovered Shane had all kinds of symptoms he hadn't mentioned.

"Are you having trouble with your speech?"

"I can't sing anymore."

Three years and thirteen weeks earlier, in a small wilderness church that looked out on the trails of Baldy Mountain, Shane had sung to me from the balcony. At the altar soared a huppah, its posts entwined in roses.

Together, by the side, stood the rabbi-emeritus from Israel and the United Church minister from Shane's childhood, who'd agreed to officiate the shared ceremony. I walked down the aisle on the arm of my mother and, under the canopy at the altar, turned around and looked up at the balcony. There stood Shane, in his black tuxedo and royal blue shirt, open at the collar, gazing down at me. A capella, he sang, "*You fill up my senses, light a light in a forest, like the mountains in springtime, like a walk in the rain. . . .*

"*Come let me love you. Let me give my life to you. Let me drown in your laughter. Let me die in your arms.*" It was the last line that repeated now.

"What about secretions," the doctor asked.

"I have a phlegm buildup I can't get rid of."

"Have you fallen?"

"Three times," Shane said.

I remembered each fall vividly. On the first, he had been racing down the stairs to say goodbye before he charged off to work, and bam! he collapsed in a heap.

Walking has become frightening, he admitted. His balance was so bad he felt he could fall anytime.

ALS can be overwhelming, the neurologist acknowledged. He seemed unaware we didn't have a diagnosis, nor know that a neuromuscular specialist meant an expert in motor neuron disease. Shane didn't even know what ALS was.

Late that night, Shane opened my office door. His face had the look it had when he told me about his brother, long and slack and inutterably sad. Behind his half-closed eyelids was a dark, dark tunnel whose end I couldn't see. "You've been reading," I said.

"Yes."

I held out my arms and he stepped into them. "I'm so scared, Liv."

I wrapped my arms around him tighter. The suffering of this disease would terrify a general.

"I don't think I can do this, Liv."

Arms around each other, the two of us cry.

In Jeanne's next session, the money issue returned.

"It's the hundred grand," she said.

"There's a problem with it?"

"It's so much money." Her whisper had the awed quality money seems to evoke.

"Are you worried about the money?"

Not at all. Her patron was a fat cat from up on Duck Mountain across the bay, where the speculators lived. A regular, he paid her in envelopes thick with cash or with money orders signed by an officer of a bank she didn't know. He'd already showed her fifty thousand smackeroonies: he had it all right, it was nothing to him, no more than a bottle of champagne or a limo ride to a poor dude. His tastes could get a little weird, but not very. He liked her to dress in a pleated plaid skirt or navy jumper and to shave her pubes and cream 'em soft as baby skin; sometimes he asked her to shout with pain and then stifle the volume to whimpery sounds, like a mewling alley cat, only softer and scared-er, which made him whacko, big as a snake, and long too, like he could thump right up to her heart and out her throat. Anything extra added money by the C-note.

"Violence, then?"

She shook her head. S & M was not his game. He never had the rape'n'kill look she'd come to know before she even hit the streets.

I couldn't fathom what the problem was.

"He wants my daughter."

All along, I'd had this uneasy feeling that I knew something I wasn't supposed to know, and now I knew what it was. Jeanne was training her daughter for the life. In my world, this was child abuse and if I didn't report it to the authorities, I could lose my license. Not a word of Jeanne's subjective world would be worth a damn in court, no matter which one of us swore to it. Retrospectively, I think this was the moment I decided to leave the practice of psychotherapy, when I understood that if my interpretation of reality didn't jibe with convention, I had to jettison what I knew. The end of subjectivity was the end of the only kind of truth that could steer a life, truth rooted in self-discovery, the stark naked truth generated by the guts.

Don't tell me what you're doing with your daughter unless you want your ass in the slammer and your kid raised in a foster home, I ranted to myself. Up until then, I would have warned her off or even reported her, if her story had contained any explicit sexual contact. Now all I said was, what's the problem.

"She's too young," Jeanne whispered. "She's only nine, she hasn't come of age. I haven't even started to teach her."

"Can't you tell him to wait?"

"He wants her like this. He keeps upping the price."

"Beyond a hundred grand?"

"He could set me up for life."

"God."

"Both of us."

"But something bothers you."

She rocked back and forth. Clad in a sheathe of shimmering silk, her foot jiggled a frantic rhythm. She was trancing out. I could see it in her eyes. The conflict was unbearable.

"I could never work another day of my life." Reverence infused her voice.

I thought you liked the life, I wanted to fling, but that was my issue. What she needed was to articulate her doubt. Something bothers you, I repeated.

"My little peaches pie."

"Your peaches."

"She's only ten."

"Nine, I thought you said."

"Ten next month."

"Her age. It bothers you."

"I haven't trained her." She was gasping for breath. It was hard to birthe the words.

One more sentence, I thought, desperate to find the trigger. "And if she's not trained and you agree to the deal . . . " I let my voice trail off.

"She'll be ruined. Her whole life, gone, in one instant." Jeanne started to cry, the same desolate wail she'd begun with. I realized I was sitting with that rare person who accepted the full strength of her emotions. That was what sex did; it opened up the abundance of experience. And that's what Jeanne was contemplating taking away from her daughter. For money. For the empty specter of material existence. I said as much, though in a murmur.

"It'd be horrible. She'd view sex as a degradation. She'd turn into a common street slut, the kind your Max thinks we all are." She spat out the victim word. "And if she ever got married, all that godgiven lust would back up in her, and she'd lie there, passive as a plank, angry with her husband's clumsy loving, unable to do a thing about it. Horrible. Oh, I don't care if she picks the life, fourth generation or not. If some other life turns her crank, that's fine, but I want her to have all the crazy wells of passion that's passed down the female side of our family, the one thing that can drive her to the tippy peak of adventure in everything she does."

"Does that answer your question, then?"

"I don't know," she said, the awe of fortune in her whisper. "We could never have to work again."

The last time I rode along with Max we passed Jeanne's corner and no one was there. Down the street, in the busy zone, where the tired old hookers peddled their cheap wares, I thought I saw a silhouette piled high with dark curls and a slender young girl, shivering in a fox fur jacket, clutching the curve of her elbow. "Go back!" I screamed to Max. "Go 'round the block." When we got back, there was nothing but the shadow of two saplings, planted as part of the city's effort to gentrify the area.

The ridealongs with Max drew to a close. Max's partner came back, hot to hit the streets, and I left my job at the Institute of Justice to take a job in another city.

Coming back from a walk, the contemplative kind I take since my husband relinquished the attempt to labor up and down the uneven slopes of our neighborhood, a battered brown Mercedes pulls alongside of me. Seated at the wheel is Fred Wilson, his charming smile a little anxious, tremulous around the lower lip. Across from him, in the passenger seat, is an Asian woman, beautiful and aging, sixty-ish I would guess, around the same age as Fred.

"Have you met my wife?" Fred asks.

I step over to the car and cant into the window, squeezing my eyes to blink away the sun.

"Mikki," Fred says. "Mikayo."

"I'm Livia," I say, smiling on top of my surprise. "Pleased to meet you at last."

Mikki's face is puffy and tired. Under skillful layers of makeup, her skin is the bruised brown of an Asian pear. Her wide lips seem a little swollen beneath the bronzy crimson lipstick, though her eyelids are painted as blue as a screensaver. "I love your garden," she says, revealing a set of slightly crooked teeth that could explain the swollen look of her lips.

"Me too," I grin. Her eyes meet mine then dart away, and something about the upswing, when the deep brown iris almost disappears, reminds me of Jeanne.

"Well, good luck to you," Fred calls. "Sure hope you get those boys to finish soon."

As they pull away, I have an enormous sensation of distance and I realize I don't feel responsible for either the brutality or the love between them. A gulf has fallen open between me and caring, and it feels very different from the way I felt about Jeanne and the daughter I wanted desperately to save. Compassion takes energy and I am tired, so very tired.

From nowhere, the image of the spacious rain that was falling the night Jeanne came to talk to me returns, and makes me think of Shane's tears, rolling and sliding down his long, sad face the night the neurologist said the words ALS. And life feels like that slow slanted rain that carries on its downward spiral towards the absorbent earth so many images: a fjord on the coast of Jeanne's British Columbia, the cedar-scented trail up Tahquitz Mountain, the deer harvesting sound in their cocked ears, the translucent feathers of a red-tailed hawk soaring circles above the canyon, the dark, polished gleam of Shane's abandoned office furniture, the puffy bruised skin of Fred's wife Mikki, the blubbery pink face of the officer in his patrol car, the omniscient eye of the boat in the harbor, Shane singing love to me from the church balcony, all of it dropping in wet, spinning dreamlets toward the thirsty ground. And I search my heart for the acceptance I've read about, but it doesn't come.

Message from Ayshah

From: ayshah72@etisalat.com
Subject: Ahlayn!!!!!
Date: December 18, 2001, 8:36 p.m.
To: emma.magsolace@securenet.com

Welcome!!!!!

I was never so excited in my life as the day my father told me he was hiring an American *woman* to run his new business. And she was to be on equal footing as a director with my brother Samir! Samir was not happy, in fact he was furious. He flushed to a bruised purple and stayed that way throughout the evening.

My nervous system electrified like a hot wire fence, sending little zinging feelings crackling through me, until even my liver trembled, my kidney, my heart, though I tried to conceal my elation. I wish they would send *me* to school in England; I'd come back broadened. I am proud of my father. No one else in this fossilized country would dare do such a thing, except my father. He is so cool, don't you think? The first with new ideas, technology, change. I wanted to throw my arms around him, but of course I didn't because I am seventeen and my father is a man.

Though I wish, sometimes, he would listen to me.

I've dreamt about you. Emma Solace. What a funny name. I looked it up in my English dictionary. "Solace:

To console. To make cheerful. To amuse." I thought, she will make me laugh. My mother claims I shouldn't laugh because something bad will happen, but you, Emma Solace, laugh in your picture, your mouth wide open like you could swallow the world, your hair the color of moonlight on water, frothy like a whipped-up sea, and completely uncovered. The top button on your blouse undone so anyone can see the milky skin on your chest covered with freckles like specks of gold in the sand.

I sneaked your visa down to the tourist photo shop where I could get a copy of that picture. The very look of it declares independence; what I *will* have in my life. Idolatry is a sin, my mother would say, quoting our Imam, because it distracts from devotion to God, but what she really fears is less respect for the family. Even my father, who is probably the most influential person in this country, not counting the royals, had to get special permission to put a statue in front of his new building, a Bedouin with a camel. So I figured the sin was small enough to be worth the risk. After all, you had the photo taken yourself. It wasn't as if I were stealing a piece of your soul. Not that I'd mind. I think you must have a soul of steel to come to Arabia all by yourself.

I take out the photo and stare at it every day. I have memorized every line on your face, even the tiny ones that look like sandpiper tracks by the sea. It is a lived-in kind of face, beautiful but homey, as if the person wearing it got weatherbeaten from being so real all the time. I try to learn from those eyes. To look into the secret parts of myself for knowledge is power and I need all the power I can get. When I gaze into your eyes, aqua like a sundrenched sea and set so far apart they can watch every direction, I feel an acceptance of things I can't say to anyone. I plunge further into myself, deeper into the murk of rage and desire. I hear myself shouting with anguish. No, I won't! I won't follow the unjust laws of God or man! I won't obey my parents! I won't be forced to marry! I won't obey God or Muhammad his Prophet and Messenger (Blessed be his name). Emma Solace is from an atheist country; her eyes permit this terrible doubt, forbidden here, punishable under charges of apostasy, yet my father doubts, he doubts and together with curiosity it has enabled him to develop and progress, to become wealthy; he doubts but he won't let me. But I *will* go to school and develop my mind, I *will* select a career and push it as far as I can. If I can't do what I want in this pathetic country I will emigrate to Where I Can.

And listen to me, listen. I won't have children. No children.

I want my eyes to behold a thousand mountains, my ears to hear a thousand tongues, my mind to rove as far as strong minds can launch it, to the stars and to Europe and to the United States of America. I want to see London and San Francisco and Paris and live in New York. In New York at Columbia University, where my father went, I will learn everything there is to know. I will wear slinky dresses and date men who hand me glasses of wine and tilt through the air between us just to hear what I have to say. My skin will feel the wetness of snow and sheets of rain, my ears will hear the timpani of thunder and the melody of harps and flutes, my lips will be kissed. I will eat pork in restaurants and go out with Jews. I will get a doctorate in the history of infidel ideas and work at the United Nations or at a university.

The eyes in your photograph understand. They say, yes, Ayshah bint Khalid bint Maryam Al Rashid you can go to Europe and America. You are smarter than Samir or Abbas or your sister Nurah, fleet of wit like your father. It hurts to neglect a brilliant mind. It hurts to chain it forever to a common mind or to expose it to no more than gossip and the swish of silk dresses. You can get a doctorate in any subject you choose, those eyes of iron assert. You can marry whoever you want.

My thoughts are so vivid I think they have happened. If I hear an interesting story about a man I instantly dream about how he might brush my hand or my neck and I feel this liquid in my body that makes me want to rock myself. I recite verses of the Qur'an to remind myself about what happens to bad women, but I think badness is a barrier to keep men away from women's souls and my thoughts just get stronger. Like last night when my father said to tomato-faced Samir, "The cowboy had another great idea." The Cowboy. That salty admiration in my father's voice. The sizzle of Samir's envy. The choice of a man is the choice of how to live. Emma of the oasis eyes will be able to answer my questions about differences between men. I must know if this liquid feeling is love, if every man can set it off or only the right one. If who I choose will matter or if all men will be uninterested in the depths of my being. I must know if a woman's life is better alone.

For months I have pondered what to offer so we can become friends (and now at last you are here!). My father must respect you immensely to hire you to manage a branch of his business. He claims you have romantic silly notions about the desert and the Badu, but a surprising amount of real knowledge too. He says you are a Catholic Christian. I guess that means you believe in some kind of god (but surely not without thought? not absolutely?). Everyone here thinks that the reason there is so much robbing and killing in the big cities of the west is because they believe Man is more important than God.

I wonder how love grows if you don't believe in God.

I wonder if doubt incapacitates love.

God. Love. Ideas. There is so much I need to talk to you about.

My father refused to let me go to the airport when you arrived. I argued with him, but he had decided. "You are not to go. You will go to school. You can meet her later when she's not so exhausted. After she's had a chance to settle." "After you've decided if I should!" I accused. "It's because I'm a girl. You're taking Abbas and Samir." "They are out of school," he said. He was lying. He did not ask Nurah and she is out of school. But Nurah didn't care if she went to the airport or met Emma Solace the American at all. Nurah only cares about music. It's like she's not even in the family.

"I'm going to live Where I Can Go to the Airport by Myself," I muttered, though not loud enough for him to hear. My mother heard. "He is trying to do what is best for you," she insisted.

If I hear those words one more time, I am going to slap her. Why does she have to perfume everything he says? He's not right all the time. And she has her own ideas. I can see them in her eyes. Once, just once, I want to hear what she thinks, not what he does. You'd think he was Allah and she was his Prophet. I started making as if to prostrate in front of her and she yanked me upright by my shoulder. "Oh, Mother," I sniveled. "How could he leave me out?" She put her arms around me like I was a little girl again.

But she didn't take my side.

The minute she left, I whipped back to this e-mail to you. Here's what I can do. I can show you underground happening Arabia, the cafés where girls go, the music and video clubs, the secret gatherings where we discuss reform, everything you will never find in books or on your own. Dearest Emma, I have a journal full of letters. I have been writing to you for months. Meet me for coffee at the Sultanah Café.

If you are hurt because my parents reneged about your staying with us, understand it is because of me. My father wants to make sure you are a fit companion for his precious daughter. Since you're not married, he's afraid that you may have turned into one of those flirty, sexy types or become discontented and bossy. He'll send you right back on the next plane if he doesn't approve of you. I'd absolutely die if that happened.

My mother worries your reputation will suffer if you live alone, but she completely panics – goes nutsie with prayer – over the thought that Samir will fall for you. She thinks he's obsessed with English women since he was at Oxford. As if marrying an upper class blonde with skinny lips would get back at all the men who snubbed him because he was Arab and brown. And you know what? I don't think it was the prejudice that offended him. I think it was the way sin is so cool there.

The day you came, I put on my favorite abayah and went to school. The abayah felt especially heavy and hot, like a gag over my whole body. I kept imagining what you would be wearing when you stepped into view. You would be dressed in pastels, as you were in your picture, strong colors that conjure images of rainbows and sunsets. The kind of colors that sparkle from crystals and sunlit water. The colors of nuance and doubt, of life lived at its most supple.

And I would be covered in black. The color of limousines and stars that disappear, of newsprint on the *Khaleej Times* and the ropes around my father's white ghutrah. The color of oil and thirst-swollen tongues. Of shadows and midnight and the unknown. Of death and slavery and domination.

The color of Gulf women.

The Dying Husbands Dinner Club

On my way into the *Mozambique* restaurant, a peach-colored parrot, hanging upside down on the outside of his cage, squawked jarringly at me. I looked at him, his scaly claws clutching the bars of his home, his belongings a cluttered mess at the bottom of the gilded enclosure, his downy peach wings folded and still, negotiating his world from a topsy turvy position, and thought, I know how you feel buddy. I threaded my way through the bar, a semi-enclosed rooftop terrace furnished in black, black and more black, scanning for a familiar face and not spotting Bronnie. Already wretched at the idea of sharing stories with three other women whose husbands had crossed the great divide from the kingdom of the well to the kingdom of the sick, all the chic black gloom made me want to run. *Everyone who is born holds dual citizenship,* Susan Sontag had written when she named the kingdoms. What she neglected to mention was that when one person got ill, the whole family migrated.

I sat at the bar for a while. They had a dry Sauvignon Blanc from Marlborough that I drank, balancing its effect with water. Around me, weedy California blondes with implanted breasts and tautened faces flirted languidly with aging surfer boys in banker suits and loosened ties. My body hunched involuntarily over the high bamboo bar. In other circumstances, I would have been drawn to these women: Bronwyn, a politician, Fredda a doctor, Grace a psychoanalyst, but now I didn't want to hang out with other women whose husbands were dying. I didn't trust them to have the moxie or whatever it took to face the horror and rage of the truth.

The sun was beginning to set, a big yellow disc in the western sky. Beyond the smooth tan stucco of a luxury hotel, the peacock sea frothed its gorgeous way towards the bluffs of the Pacific coast. Bronwyn Meade and Grace Sanchez-Hughes sat side by side on a bench of plump cushions, their backs to the south where the coast highway ran all the way from the art-rich town of Laguna Beach through Camp Pendleton Marine base into San Diego county down to the San Ysidro border crossing into Mexico. Across from them, the tall back of Fredda Rowallan rose like a portal. The sounds of early evening traffic and surf mingled into sibilance underneath the jazz and chatter of the happy people clustered in the *Mozambique* bar.

They were talking about sex when I arrived at the table. Bronnie made introductions though I already knew Fredda and had run into Grace at several art walk events. "You have to get him to change his drug," Fredda was explaining. She was a doctor and one of the husbands was using Viagra, a drug that doesn't work after six months. I never knew whose husband it was, but it made me remember a time in Mexico, in between marriages, when I'd spent a night with an old sweetheart who was using Viagra. His organ had lost its elasticity and thwacked inside me like a corn cob.

Coming to the table had sobered me up, so I ordered a second glass of Sauvignon Blanc, though I wasn't a very good drinker and was already feeling hazy. As we ordered salads and dishes with peri-peri sauce, the house specialty, it struck me that all of us concentrated hard on the menu and I wondered if this was a woman thing or if food had become a matter of grave concern because it was our only pleasure.

The discussion about sex continued, Bronnie arch about how no sex on top of cleaning her husband's urinal was too much. With pouty pink lips, hair as pale as the noonday sun, and a sprinkle of mustache down above her upper lip, Bronnie could get away with being arch about anything. Beside her, delicately drinking a robust-looking red, Grace was also beautiful: flames of hair dyed saucy auburn, subtle greens in her fine-featured face suggesting malaise or fragility; an artistic beauty. Tall and lithe, Fredda was all body and energy, everything about her conveying earth and sense.

I thought about sex with Shane, remembering the early days, when his erection was constant, and I thought I'd finally found a man who could give as much as he took. On a mountain near his hometown, there were outdoor hot tubs in secluded shelters and we booked one on a midnight in June. Outside the stars massed bright and low, dangling a galactic halo above us as we walked along a dark trail behind an attendant carrying fluffy white towels. Inside, skin pressed against skin, we floated in the liquid massage of the water until my legs drifted around him and he swam into me. Looking down the dark slope at the pinpoint lights of the city and up at the massed

Julie Brickman

starlight, I felt the rhythm of love flow upward, hot liquid outside and in, and in those moments knew bliss. Like a graceful hawk, Shane's erection soared that night, making what felt like swooping circles in the canyon of my flesh, and now it was the only part of him except his mind that worked like it used to: his legs couldn't hold him up over me, his hands lacked the agility for feathery caresses; a grounded hawk, he was now.

Across the table, Bronwyn elbowed Grace. "Bet Finn's still a dish." A rosy pink curled fingers around Grace's white throat and she gave her wine a blank hard look.

I poked at my barren mound of flaccid spring greens, dull as John Updike, and watched Bronnie spear fleshy strips of seared ahi tuna and insert them through the perfect oh of her round pink lips. When the last strip was down, she patted the sesame oil from her pout, smiled brightly, and I swear it was like the sun had landed in the middle of our table.

"Girls!" Bronwyn raised her glass. Her wine looked like moonlight.

Our glasses formed a circle above the table: magenta, cherry, yellow, gold asparkle in the fading light.

"The Dying Husbands Club," Bronnie laughed prettily. "That's what my husband said when I left the house tonight. 'You're going to your Dying Husbands Dinner Club.'"

The irony was comforting, like a bruising workout, particularly since it came from a dying husband. We toasted to our name.

"We should fill Livia in on what's happening with our husbands," Bronnie said.

"Ah, girls," Fredda sighed. "Tonight let's just enjoy ourselves."

This we all knew was impossible, though the yearning in me burned so fierce it felt like annihilation. Here I was in the one group where I didn't have to explain how I was taking care of myself (which I wasn't) or keeping my spirits buoyed (which I couldn't) or finding some upside to misery (which there wasn't), and maybe, just maybe, I could let myself be real for a change.

I punched the air with my glass. "Something profound always comes out of suffering. That's what a friend of mine said the other day."

"Bet you wanted to pound the goo out of that conversation," Grace drawled.

Bronwyn laughed through her sunlight smile. "Try church. There you get, God doesn't give us more than we can bear. Along with, you are in my prayers."

"I get the flaky cures." A burst of laughter flared through Fredda's nostrils. "You know, my friend Joe the dogcatcher had the exact same symptoms and he went to a doctor in Costamexicuba who gave him a treatment of gluconeurothingy and now he's completely better."

Into her blasé soft voice, Grace injected faux sympathy. "Have you tried massage? Meditation? Yoga? *Sleep*?" Like a discordant musical phrase, her laugh was tinkly and bitter.

The restaurant's dinner plates were curved into half-bowls and elevated on wide stems, elegant and yet somehow trough-like. I leaned down, and sucked a juicy morsel right into my mouth. "There," I muttered. "That's my answer to *there's always something good to come out of suffering.*"

Grace contorted her delicate features but gave a soft laugh.

"Just can't take her anywhere," Bronnie said.

"What d'you do that for?" Fredda asked.

"Because all the clichés and niceties people deliver are cruel. Because my world is raw and ugly and I don't want to lie about it. The one thing I've found is this weird kind of freedom." I leaned down again.

"Whoa!" Bronnie called, but Fredda leaned with me. She sucked in a vegetable, little snorts peppering the breathy sound, and no one complained because Fredda was a doctor and had prestige, but I could feel myself sinking, the breathiness reminding me of the whoosh-whoosh of Shane breathing on a ventilator. Somewhere in the mélange I heard Fredda say, "No more pretending."

Bronwyn downed a whole glass of wine. "I'm an alcoholic!" She gave her pretty laugh. "I drink a whole bottle while I'm making dinner."

"I buy art," Grace said. "Every week, a new piece. I'm going through our savings as fast as Finn."

I confessed to picking fights with strangers. "Sometimes I go out and say something deliberately rude or mean. And it makes me feel better."

"Like what?" Distaste tinged Grace's soft voice.

I shrugged. "The other day I asked a barista at a coffee shop when she gained so much weight."

Surprisingly, Grace giggled, though she tacked on a grimace. Bronwyn turned an inquiring look to Fredda, who shrugged impishly. "Does sports count?"

"Walter couldn't be that ill," Bronnie said.

It jolted me, her casual remark. Because of the truth in it. Walter wasn't that ill. Nor was Keith, nor Finn. Shane was the only husband who'd stopped working. The only one whose house had been remodeled, complete with ramps, platform elevators, raised toilets, grab bars, commercial carpet, roll-in shower, hospital bed. Gone were the buttery yellow living room sofas, the translucent coffee table, the easy chairs. Gone was the oval glass dining table, the multi-colored French dining chairs, the ability to entertain friends at dinner or parties; gone the shelves of books, speakers, photographs; in their place tubing, batteries, assistive devices, failed hopes, ransacked dreams, loneliness, the odor of dying.

Under domes of hazelnut ice cream, our warm potted chocolate cakes arrived and we dug into them. Bronnie ordered a dessert wine for all of us and said, insistently this time, "We really should fill Liv in." By now, inebriation and a pinch of hysteria had lent our woes an outlandish edge.

Bronwyn's husband Keith had aggressive Parkinson's. Five years the doctor had told her, taking her aside on her last visit.

"It's amazing how well he handles it. Last weekend at the opera, people came up behind him and carped at him to get a move on. Well, he just turned around and told them straight out, I have Parkinson's and I'm moving as fast as I can."

"You still go to the opera?" I couldn't remember the last time Shane and I had gone out. Probably to a restaurant, the Indian one in our neighborhood where we'd once eaten regularly, seated side by side, across from

61

two vacant chairs, brushing into each other's yielding warmth. That last night, we'd ordered dishes that were soft, for Shane's jaw muscles could no longer grind up chunks of meat or chicken, but not until the hot cheese and potatoes slid out of his mouth did we realize how much his lips had slackened.

Bronnie's glance trolled the little forest of wine glasses beside each of our plates. I passed her my dessert wine and her shoulders shuddered into a slump. So much she wasn't going to tell us was in that slump – revulsion, sorrow, defeat, fear. We saw it all and had nothing to give her. Bronwyn had married the man who had everything. Six foot four, bearded, black and silver-haired, classically handsome Keith – neurosurgeon and former marine – now ambulated in jerky, toddler-sized steps, completely at odds with his large serious bearing. By day, he wielded a dark polished cane, but at night at home, he pushed a silver walker and peed in a urinal he kept beside his bed. Yeah, they still went to the opera.

"It's Walter's face that gets me." Fredda's zest had receded. "There's nothing on it. His body language and facial cues are kaput. It's like living with a zombie." Multiple system atrophy caused rigidity, not just of the gait but all over the body: arms too stiff to bend; torso frozen, face expressionless. "And his mind!" Neutrality flattened her tone and she sounded clinical. "It's getting as rigid as his body." Unlike most neurological disorders, MSA was painful. Walter's back and legs were riddled with cramps; he flailed and jerked his way through the nights, sometimes thumping Fredda with an arm or a leg.

A rare look of interest spiced Grace's face. Her pointy breasts – no implants there – nearly grazed the rim of her wine glass as she slanted towards Fredda. "Have you let him know he's losing it?"

"Poor Walter. No, he'll find out soon enough at work. He's so slow, he can't possibly carry his share much longer."

Grace rocked back against her chair. Something was sliding around her face besides boredom, letdown or maybe hurt. Finn was losing it: he had frontal-temporal lobe dementia, neurologically-based insanity.

Basically, people with FTD became crazy. They lost control and became impulsive, not blurt-impulsive, but spend-all-the-savings impulsive, brawl-in-bars impulsive: manic, euphoric and witless. Worst of all, Finn had no capacity for empathy; no ability to imagine his effect on anyone. Not that he'd had much empathy before, Grace added. Fredda wanted to know how long since Grace had noticed the changes.

"Five years ago, I think. It's subtle. I wasn't sure at first."

"Subtle?" A fragile word, too quiet to describe a violent dementia. Since I'd become a writer, I preferred my words and people on the page, where I could relax in their company, not like now when I was drinking too much and feeling tense as a borderline.

"Grace is an opera singer," Bronwyn announced. "She's sung in the chorus at Opera Pacific."

"Is that right?!" I noticed a slight alteration in my opinion of Grace: less wariness, more interest; the word subtle no longer an issue. Talent always upended my sense of values.

Grace said Finn's mood swings made him vicious and her urge to be cruel in return plundered her self-image, was, as she put it, ego-dystonic.

"It eats at you, doesn't it," I muttered to Grace. There was nothing like illness to show you how small you could be, to highlight every personal shortcoming in lurid neon like a cheap sign. So many of mine were surfacing toward Shane. A red light district of faults.

Grace's eyes filled with tears, turning them a seaweed green. "What eats at me is how little money there is left for me to ditch him."

Grace's hair poked out in little spiky things that no longer looked chic. Nor did her suit: tiny geometric shapes superimposed on plaid fabric; totally garish. Irritability was the basic sign of life, my scientist father used say, his blue Semitic eyes twinkling as he pointed out that I was *very alive*. But I didn't feel alive. I just felt lonely again, untethered to the women around me. My way of processing the world had changed since I'd become a writer. I wanted to know what Finn *did*. How he smelled. What he loved about deep sea fishing.

Grace was worried about the mortgage, about having enough savings to look after herself when she was old. It made me realize how savvy these women were, how able to cherish their own futures, how different from me, spending down my capital to look after Shane. ALS, according to an article I'd seen in the *Journal of the American Medical Association*, was the most expensive disease on the planet, costing an average of two hundred thousand a year in gear and care, sucking down eleven hours a day of spousal time, even with hired help. At least Finn had been squandering his own money on carousing, or so Grace implied, though once, when he'd come back stinking of dirty linen and expensive perfume, Grace had questioned him and he'd flung his shaver (a Braun, the cord attached) at the wall.

Finishing our decaffeinated coffees (Grace had caffeine), everyone got up to leave. We were sated from the sadness of Keith, the torment of Walter, the danger of Finn.

At our second dinner, sitting round a table under the high dark beams and dangle of shadowy lights at the *Sapphire* restaurant, Bronwyn asked me to fill them in on Shane's illness.

I looked around at these women, Grace's spiked scarlet hair a tamed sort of crazy, Bronwyn's platinum sweet and harsh, Fredda's chestnut sculpted and short, and ran a hand through my dark curls, imagining they showed how messy and chaotic I felt inside. Shane had ALS, amyotrophic lateral sclerosis or Lou Gehrig's disease, but due to a technicality on one of his tests, his official diagnosis was PLS or primary lateral sclerosis.

"That's a hogwash diagnosis," Fredda said.

I totally agreed. By now, I could quote chapter and verse about motor neurons, which by any name were what Shane was losing. Why quibble over the label when they all meant that the brain was no longer able to control the voluntary motor systems: legs, arms, torso, lungs, speech, swallowing? As far as I was concerned it would be more descriptive to call it the scourge or the affliction than any of the medical vulgarities Shane and I spent our time reading about. Because that's what we did now, in our fifth year of marriage; we read and talked about amyotrophic lateral sclerosis. Unlike the other husbands, in denial and trying to live as they had before, Shane had made the disease his major project. "No one wants to save my life as much as I do," Shane said. "If I can't come up with a treatment, no one will."

The women thought this was terribly responsible of Shane. Futile as they acknowledged it was. Shane's disease was incurable; the most effective drug slowed its course by two months.

I remembered the first meeting I'd attended of people with ALS – PALS as they are nauseatingly called. Shane had just told me he felt like he was drowning or suffocating when he tried to get enough air, and that week the ALS association had a respiratory therapist as a speaker. There were about two dozen people in the room, half of them in wheelchairs, and in the front was a display of face masks: clear plastic molds, designed to cover all or part of the face, attached to fat breathing tubes, like elephant trunks, that coiled their way over to a ventilator, a machine that functioned like an external lung. About ten minutes into the presentation, excitement rustled through the room, and in came The Woman Whose Husband Had Had ALS for Eighteen Years. She was desperately thin, clothed entirely in black. The husband lay back in his wheelchair, a large modular Permobil, tilted into the angles of a W. Beside his black-garbed, immobile shape, a caregiver maneuvered the joystick while someone else rolled medical equipment in on a cart. He was physically *locked-in,* unable to move even a muscle, powerless to communicate his wishes even through the assistance of an eye- or brain-stimulated cursor.

"Livia!" Bronnie wanted to know what Shane's first symptom was.

"His foot. It dragged. And he said right away, *My left foot won't do what my brain tells it.* He knew it was in his brain."

When we were first married, I used to listen to the movement of his feet as though it were music. They'd clatter; they'd thump; they'd tap; they'd race. And I'd sit in my office, at the bottom of the house, my heart keeping time, wondering how I got so lucky. "We met hiking, you know. I was an outing leader for the Sierra Club. He was a peak climber and a runner, had climbed fourteeners all over the country. Me, I'd have to look down when the trails got rocky and there he'd be, gazing out at the scenery, strolling along. I mean, we hiked up Tahquitz in Idyllwild and Vernal Falls in Yosemite, him with a dropped foot on that one. Oh God."

I missed that Shane. Every day, I heard him clunk around on the walker and thought of the Shane who would amble up the rocky slopes behind me, pointing out wild flowers, tiptoeing behind deer. In the old days, we'd hike the Elfin Forest or another steep trail until we felt *the change* when only the sensory existed: the crunch of our footsteps on earth and rocks, the yellow of the monkey flowers, the stir of the breeze, the brown and green cup of the valley, the meadows. Now he barely stayed upright as he took one ponderous step after another on the rehabilitation treadmill, the red stop cord wrapped around his wrist. Once, I found him crumpled up on the sofa beside the elliptical, sobbing. I can't get my heart rate up, he freaked.

"*My foot won't do what my mind tells it*, that really captures it, doesn't it?" The authority in Fredda's voice implied the sentences to come. My hand won't do what my mind tells it. My throat won't do what my mind tells it. My lungs won't do what my mind tells them.

"Keith freezes on the way to the bathroom," Bronnie said. "I have to push him started, then he can walk. I used to cry every night."

I still do, I thought, wondering if I'd ever stop. Life was pocked by losses, accumulating into small voids, like my unwritten stories, the ache of them.

I pushed my plate away, suddenly sickened by the jiggling brown pudding. A bison-faced thug had tried to kill me in a dream the night before and I told them how just as he was about to slash, I yelled to my dreaming self, wake up wake up, it's the only way to live.

"The conflict between living and dying," Grace said. "Dreams are beautiful like that."

"I'm not sure I want to hear about it," Bronnie said, pouting but looking adorable.

"I guess that's what we have to look forward to," Fredda mused.

But I wasn't going to tell them all I really knew. The other Sunday, as I crawled under Shane's shower chair to wash his shit-smeared anus, I thought, *spare me the horror of this wretched life, die already* about the person I loved more than anyone in the world. "Does anyone yearn to get out?" I ventured.

"All the time," Grace said. "If Finn's mother still wants him, I'm going to pack him right off to Florida." She eye-cruised the next table and two of the men sent her sly, provocative looks.

Bronwyn gave an artless little shudder. "I pray God won't make Keith suffer too much. I pray every night."

A meditative look creased Fredda's face and I almost thought she knew the darkness. She said was going to put Walter in a home when his mind was gone.

"Enough! Here's to traveling!" Bronnie lifted her empty glass. She and Keith had trips planned to Patagonia, Japan and Fiji. Grace was going to Costa Rica and Fredda to Ireland.

I didn't bother to mention what held me at home, how this tenderness towards Shane just appeared, like a surge from some better being. It had nothing to do with character, for I knew myself to be an impatient person with plenty of mean impulses. But there was this thing that happened, this almost intolerable yearning to protect the person I watched suffering every day, this grinding ache in my heart; or soul, for soul had never seemed like a part of myself whose actions I could consciously claim. For I would see the fasciculations rattle Shane's legs while he slept, notice the concentration he exerted just to tap the keyboard with his one mobile hand. In my sleep, I am whole, he told me.

"Does anyone else dream of another lover?" Bronwyn asked, her aqueous eyes naughty over the rim of the coffee cup.

Fredda flexed a fit arm. "Of course."

"I'll be too spent," I said, for still I only dreamt of Shane.

"Nonsense." Fredda bristled, all doctor again. "The fifties are the best years. And the sixties. You really have a rich sense of life but you haven't started to decline. Even the seventies can be harvest years."

"Have any of you *dated* recently?" I said, a snicker rising, though it wasn't dates they needed, but dreams.

"God, no," said Bronwyn. "I've been married thirty-two years."

"Twenty," said Fredda.

"Thirteen," Grace murmured. "This time."

"Ah. What you're missing." Awful, the dating world, but better than dying husbands for humor. "First. The coffee date. There you are, standing in the doorway, scanning the room for the guy who told you he's six feet tall with a blond beard and an athletic build. No one by that description in the room. Maybe you should sit down, by yourself. But no, there's someone nodding at you from the corner. A fat guy with a grey beard, five-seven, maybe five-eight. He's described who he used to be many years ago, in his *fantasies*, which means he still thinks of himself as thirty. Which also means he thinks *you* look like his mother and are not even slightly sexy."

Grace had the rosy necklace materializing. "I went into an internet site," she murmured. "I don't want to wait."

"Did you, like . . . ?" Bronwyn's eyes were huge.

"We could advertise," I bantered. "The Dying Husbands Dinner Club seeks men over forty, whose wives have fatal diseases, for discreet dinners. Neurological ailments preferred." The joke made me feel like a cad.

Which I was, I reflected on the way home. Not that this had been a willing recognition. Years ago, in one of my transitional phases, I had gone through a period where I'd identified with every fool and villain in any book I read. In *Pride and Prejudice*, I'd identified not with the brilliant Elizabeth nor the beautiful Jane, nor even with the wanton Lydia, but with crass, klutzy Mary, who thought she had more musical talent than she did. In *A Walk in the Woods*, instead of fit, knowledgeable, hilarious Bryson I identified with fat, wheezing, inept, treat-gobbling Katz. In *Song of Solomon*, it was irritable, critical, domineering Macon Dead.

It had been a labyrinth of self-discovery, but it was nothing compared to this. There I was in the company of women I thought would need coddling and it turned out they were all much fiercer than I. We had sat with each other tonight, exploring all the ways we could leave our husbands, but I knew I never would. I didn't have that brand of toughness, the ruthlessness that made others around me craft something valuable of their lives. All I could do was gaze into the deepening darkness and watch the urge to evil and the urge to empathy spring from same desperate moments; to live out the lonely incommunicable experience of loving a husband who was dying slowly, too slowly for my weary compassion, aware that others might make the choice to leave when it became unbearable, but that I would make the choice to bear the yearning. And I thought about people whose darkness was greater than mine, mothers and fathers who had lost their children, ordinary citizens who had witnessed torture, hungry children wandering alone in wartime, writers in gulags and daughters in brothels, and knowing they knew the darkness comforted me.

I turned into my driveway and laid my head against the steering wheel. How lovely it would be to flop down on the couch, read for a while, but my dying husband, migrating far into the interior of the kingdom of the ill, was waiting for the interlude of pleasure we still referred to as dinner. When sadness suffused me, I knew I was home.

An Empty Quarter

You never know what boundaries love will make you cross.

In the morning, you sneak into the men's quarters, slip into Samir's room. You have not been here in fourteen years, since he entered manhood. You are shocked by the change, the dark grain of the woods, the sleek blacks of the sound and video equipment. You still think of him immersed in celestial blues from pale noon to deep midnight, the colors you selected for his childhood.

You inch the door closed, slide the bolt into place. Now you can take your time. You don't feel like an intruder when you search your daughters' rooms. Samir's drawers are in meticulous order, the articles squared into columns and rows. You rummage with light, cautious fingers, seeking something extraordinary or hidden. You pause in the drawer with his *iqals,* for you know headropes are precious, like jewelry, and think he might conceal something of meaning beside them. You find nothing.

You remove a *thaub* from the next drawer, inhale his lingering scent. You can still smell the baby in it, a freshness as shocking as your first mouthful of sweet water. If Paradise has a fragrance, it is that of a newborn son.

You pick through his closet, his jeans, suits, jackets, his ornate *bishts.* When he drapes one of those dark, embroidered silk cloaks over the whiteness of his *thaub*, he looks so handsome you wish he had to mask, to protect himself from the gaze of licentious women, like the American, who look at his face without being married to him. You first glimpsed your husband on your wedding day, his face like a falcon on a hunt, every haughty plane angled towards the victories he knew were to come. You knew at that moment you could surrender to such a man and to no other.

You wonder if you should search the bed, forbidden now that your son has become a man. You miss watching him sleep, checking each breath. You used to smell each exhalation, as if it were a scent from eternity, and scoot away, intoxicated and breathless.

Insubstantial, almost ethereal, you stretch across the puff of the comforter. The bed, king-sized and high off the floor, reminds you of your nights with your husband Khalid. The weave of the comforter is a blend of silk and cotton, as soft as a new bride's skin. You elongate into an angel like you once did in the cool shadowed sand. Dark paisley shapes ripple beneath you. You remember waiting in anticipation for Khalid's footsteps, your whole body one quivering ear.

On your hands and knees, you glide to the pillows, unfurl the comforter. The sheets are satin, almost luminescent, a dark shade of amber. You burrow between them. They combine the slick and the soft, like a liar's face. You inch the hem of your dress to your knees, scissor your legs along their cool surfaces. A faint smell of musk and sweat exhales from the covers. Your son's profile hovers on the screen in front of your eyelids like a giant billboard of the shaykh. Your mind kaleidoscopes into pure color.

When the colors dim you know where to look, but you don't want to move. You want to sleep in this cocoon of intimacy with your son. You have not felt this lightness in your soul, since you first held him your arms, still slick from the fluids of your own body, and as defenseless as an exposed heart. You must save him now, or try, whatever it takes. You budge one leg, as heavy as a sack of grain, and almost as limp. It is such effort, this love for your children. You will yourself to move, to search the cabinet in the bathroom you have just pictured.

The towels are stacked by size on ascending shelves. Their lemon scent reminds you of the splash of cool sparkling water on your face. You have never gotten over the joy of sweet water pouring from faucets and shower-heads, of washing and drinking whenever you please. Underneath the middle stack, you find the pamphlets you are looking for.

It is worse than you thought. The pamphlets are from political organizations, Arabian Jihad and another whose name you don't recognize, the Gulf Islamic League. You close the lid on the toilet, sit down, and read. The Jihad pamphlet cites surahs from the Qur'an. *"Think not of those who are slain in God's way as dead. Nay, they live, finding their sustenance in the presence of their Lord. (2:154)"* These look like religious documents, designed to attract people into serious Islamic study. You must have mistaken their intent.

But they quote this in the context of suicide martyrs, the kind Samir denounced as Israeli fabrications at dinner.

Here they are called missionaries, the highest and purest of the faithful, embraced by Allah in Paradise for all time. Surely your Samir is too educated to fall for this nonsense. Surely he knows that Paradise might be a fable, not a place. That if it isn't, he will reenact his heretical act forever. Is he this angry? To throw away his life? And for what? These donkey-blooded cretins, these false imams, who slithered out of a refuse heap of the world's losers to swaddle young boys in false glory?

Yes, yes, Islam can keep the world from self-destructing. Everyone you know believes that. But this is a perversion of belief, the vision of a brute or a whore. Love and power unite in a sacred state of mind. You have had glimpses, moments of such a state, where love is so vast, it embraces everyone, even infidels and westerners, even Jews, as your husband would admit, if pressed, though only to you and only in privacy. In such a state, your enemy is beautiful, his life worth more than your own, for a coveted death poisons the marrow of your being, weakens your link with God.

The brochure outlines the training of a religious warrior: elevated by his spiritual teacher for special attention and training; the envy of his peers. Alone with his mentor for hours, days, sometimes weeks, he chants and prays until he attains a transcendent state in which his thoughts dwell only on God and His Will. You cannot believe what you are reading. They take the most sacred holy state a man can attain, a moment of supreme purity when innocence and knowledge become one, and they twist and pervert it, teach people it serves God to kill, when it serves only the Devil, when it ensures their burning in Hell, if Hell is the end of your soul. You cannot allow your Samir to die, or live, in such a state.

In the final paragraph, the pamphlet extols the teaching of an exiled religious scholar, who says that death is the only time in life a real Muslim can be sure he has completely submitted to God's Will and is free of his own, for what being, without the help of God, chooses death? It outrages you that any Man thinks he knows when God's Will is pure. *It is not for any soul to believe save by the permission of Allah.*

You can't imagine why your son, who has everything, would throw away his life in such a headstrong, foolish way. You would take his place if you could. You cannot imagine dying without the thought of Samir as you go.

Your veins are gutters for the anguish that seeps from your children.

You can't find the words to pray. What kind of God accepts the sacrifice of an eldest son? You don't recognize Samir's God and your God as the same. You have been reciting Surahs in your mind all morning, but they are monotonous, unmusical. You chant and sing, trying to find your innermost being, where God dwells. It is vacant, like the heart of a mother who has a plaque of commendation in place of a son, an empty quarter. God has never been an enigma to you, but a presence strong inside you, who says His words to guide you in a loud, clear voice, bass and resonant, stronger than the song of the muezzin, and not at all like your own inner voice, which tinkles in tones higher and sweeter than when you speak. Like baklavah nubbled with pistachios, this is the voice you will have when you die.

Julie Brickman

You kneel, prostrate, try to pray on the austere little mat angled towards Makkah near the Qur'an table in the corner of the room. *Why my son?* you cry, you who have always accepted God's word without question. Take me instead. A desolation darker than the shroud of a burqah blackens the vision of life you carry inside you, blots it out. You hear nothing, neither the deep voice of God nor the tinkle of your own. Only silence, a heavy blank sound, not even viscous. Silence, and its color is black. Is this what it's like to be secular? To have no company inside?

Like cold lightning, a new and terrible chill travels through you. You understand those sad Palestinian mothers you have seen on Al Jazirah who celebrate their sons' deaths. They believe killing will restore the voice of God to their minds, justice to their lands, futures to the children of their children. In a fight to keep the darkness of *al-Gharb*, where the sun vanishes into night, from closing over their hearts, they offer their sons. Bereft, they have come to see God as a Great Housekeeper, sweeping away rubble and devastation and loss. God will clear the horror around them, reinstate love and nourishment and order. Islam will prevail once again against the chaos of *jahiliyyah*.

You snuff out these useless thoughts. You herd them into a tiny corner of your mind where you allow yourself pride in the *karamah* of a son who would rather face death than bend to the will of unbelievers who would desecrate truth. You too want modernity without decadence; you agree that the West, in its greed, has suppressed Arab progress, but Islamists use methods as corrupt at the ones they oppose. They are extremists and extremists always

78

lose. You must rescue your son from their web. You must help him find a position of moderation and reason.

You pick up the booklet from the study table where you flung it when you started to pray. "*Warfare is ordained for you, though it is hateful unto you; but it may happen that ye hate a thing which is good for you, and it may happen that ye love a thing which is bad for you. Allah knoweth, ye know not. (2:216)*"

Samir would go far to protect you – perhaps you encouraged a sense of omnipotence that prevented him from understanding the relationship between personal limits and *hudad* boundaries that are sacred – but how far? *How far would he go?*

Unlike you and Khalid, Samir hadn't seen the poverty of your country before the discovery of oil, hadn't lived in a frond hut with no running water and not enough to eat, or watched small children die from treatable flus or infections. He didn't understand that your distaste for the British had little to do with their infidel religion and everything to do with the hospitals and schools they didn't build while they filled their tankers with oil and their coffers with revenues that your people never saw. Your generation, who made the transition from privation to comfort, never saw modernity as antithetical to Islam, but his generation equates Islam with the struggles of the Prophet, Allah's blessings upon him, and rejects all that is progressive as corrupt. It has drawn them backwards towards the extremism you read in this pamphlet.

Its authors talk about atrocities directed against Muslims all over the world, which raise no outcry from so-called free governments or peoples. For this reason, they claim that the Universal Declaration of Human

Rights of the United Nations is nothing but fraudulent, hypocritical propaganda, never intended to apply to Muslims, only to Christians and Jews. America and its heathen allies have only one goal: to destroy all Muslims and obtain control of their wealth and oil. And so: "We must rain bullets and bombs against the atheists and sinners who plot to make us part of their infidel empire. We must spill their blood and bleed them of their wealth. *Those who believe do battle for the cause of Allah: and those who disbelieve do battle for the cause of idols. So fight the minions of the devil. Lo! the devil's strategy is ever weak. (4:76)*"

You used to think Samir was gifted – a child of destiny – connected in his blood and bones to the reality of others, his eyes open inside the womb, as your grand-mother would have said. You watched over him more closely than your others, worried that the cruelty of life could warp or crush him, but as his sensitivity folded into curiosity, he probed the Qur'an for dictums about justice and charity, read the work of clerics and scholars. You knew he was yearning for something, but you believed the way of scholarship was safe.

Then came the trip with his father back to New York, where you had lived in the early years of your marriage, and the endless questions it raised in his inquisitive mind. Why do they have so much – he called it life, but you knew he meant happiness, enthusiasm, *fun* – though you had seen it as a profound but inexplicable tie between people, a connectedness as deep as the *Ummah* just because they shared a terrain of pavement or grass, as if common places like parks and streets and libraries and schools could be their own as much as a house or a dress.

Everything around them *belonged* to them and they belonged everywhere they walked or drove or ate or shopped.

Why do they act as if they are important even when they are poor? Samir went on, reflective not angry, not yet. Was it because they were white? It wasn't limited to whites. Christian? But some were Muslims, Jews, even atheists. Rich? But we were rich. Maybe it was because they had a say in their government, a vote? Was it the franchise? Or the way boys his age, younger, played on the streets: ball games, bike games, games of tag, marbles, cards, checkers, chess; laughing, shouting, teasing; always making noise and always in motion? One even called out to him, hey man you wanna play ball?

For you, it had been the benches. In front of public buildings or lining the paths that crisscrossed little concrete parks they called squares were benches where anyone could sit. On benches, the rich and the poor, the white and the brown, the men and the women, *ghurabah* who were not kin, sat beside each other and chatted, without fear, about the weather or their children. You used to roam everywhere and sit on the benches, raise your eyes and drink in life. A confidence you came to think of as community, an enviable sense of being somebody in a great place, pervaded life even on the crowded jostling disorderly obscene streets of New York.

Yet Samir has come to hate the exuberance of America. Heavy-limbed and weary, you slump onto his bed, as though you had just given birth in the sand, like your mother and grandmother did beside their great tents. Your head weighted with shame, you force yourself to focus on the text in front of you, cruder than the sewage that once coursed to the sea.

The arguments are frighteningly similar to the widespread beliefs of your friends. They talk about hundreds of thousand Iraqi children wantonly killed by sanctions that deprived them of food and medicine. How in the Occupied Territories, blood and guts of women and children run down the streets, a sight you see nightly on Al Jazirah. Chechnya, Bosnia, Herzegovina, Kashmir, Somalia, Tajikistan, Afghanistan, Myanmar, the Philippines: all the wars in the world are aimed at Muslims by governments armed with American weapons and supported by funds from their infidel allies. "It is obvious," they conclude, "that the Christians are in league with the Zionist devils to pursue a Holy War, continued from the Crusades, whose goal is the eradication of the Muslim religion and the confiscation of all our Holy Lands.

How should ye not fight for the cause of Allah and of the feeble among men and of the women and the children who are crying: Our Lord! Bring us forth from out this town of which the people are oppressors! Oh, give us from Thy presence some protecting friend! Oh, give us from Thy presence some defender! (4:75)."

Footsteps thump like heartbeats and you immobilize yourself on the edge of the bed, slow your breathing to gain calm. You should not have stayed so long in the male quarters; activity increases as the day moves towards siesta. For such a transgression, you could be confined to the house and you cannot afford this when your son needs aid. The nearly inaudible sound of flipflops against carpet ambles past the doorway and down the corridor. *Bong* bong. *Bong,* bong. It is your younger son, Abbas, who favors his left leg. If you get caught, any plan is finished. You must wait now until he leaves.

You and Khalid lived in New York long before the West was an opportunity for anyone but the shaykhs and the brigands, before oil wealth had filtered down to the people. When you returned, your stories about America raised such jealousy or incredulity in your friends, you stopped telling them. But like an unsettled feud, an untold story influences everything. The American years became the core identity of your family, hijacked the imaginations of your most gifted children, your unpredictable Samir, your daring and beautiful Ayshah.

Ayshah is the only one too young to remember the experience that made you outsiders in your own culture. Her exclusion from the family's – shameful? do you feel ashamed of those years? – past has become an obsession. The spell of America enchants her. She reads fervently about New York, raids forbidden Internet sites to download music and movies, flaunts her intention to elope with an airline pilot or an officer stationed in the Gulf, acquire citizenship any way she can. Bold and flagrantly ambitious, she is just like her father. But her father had no opportunities if he did not leave the country. Things have changed since then.

This morning Ayshah was lurching around the house with something momentous on her mind, when you were trying to figure out a surreptitious way into Samir's room. You skulked around in an effort to avoid her, knowing you would be cruel if she cornered you, but, as if vision were a product of the heart, a cataract of moisture filmed over your eyes. You almost bumped into her in the corridor.

"You have to let me invite Emma out," she blurted. Her voice pleaded solo in the empty air.

"By myself."

Emma. The American. Not a good time to ask.

"To the Sultanah," she pressed. She quaked with tremors, which reminded you of dying, though you knew it was the surge of her hormones.

"Control yourself," you snapped, your own voice slapping you with its harshness. You would have to marry Ayshah off soon. Nothing else could protect her from her fascination with the West.

Her face beseeched you. She looked achingly beautiful.

"I doubt it," you replied. "But I'll give it more thought."

Ayshah's hunger for freedom blinds her to the flawed situation of western women, the restless inner chaos generated by the unsettled spirits of partial liberation. Heavy makeup; dresses as small and tight as reptilian skins; perfumed and bejeweled, as if sex might occur anytime; eyes that rake over them in fantasy without intimacy: that is their freedom. Possibilities that seem without horizons in their adolescence dwindle to naught in maturity and old age. Exactly what you don't want for your Ayshah. At least Gulf women acquire authority as they age.

It is time to concede, you dislike western women. They are arrogant in their assumption that what they call freedom makes their lives more worthy than your own.

From morning till night, western women enslave themselves to the serial fantasies of the men they encounter. They smile their whorey apologetic smiles and offer their flirty obsequious chatter to cater to every man's urges while simultaneously appeasing his rage at not getting what he wants. And if that isn't enough, they are surrounded – assaulted! – by a procession of magazine and television images that exalt and idealize the lowest, most degraded forms of male desires, until these free western women have no moments in their days when they can burrow inside themselves deeply enough to hear their own voices, much less that of God.

Every day you give thanks that you were born a Muslim woman, that you can go out in your protective raiments and just be yourself. A predictable set of fantasies are at the helm of your life, not the endless babble western women must sift and distinguish from their authentic interior thoughts every day. You cannot imagine how they ever feel stable inside.

Samir seemed preoccupied with instability last night at dinner when he announced that the security system in the new office didn't seem safe enough for an agency that served western expatriates and tourists.

"You think we'll be a target?" Abbas, your quiet son, asked.

"Remember Egypt?" Samir said. "The fifty-eight foreign tourists al-Gama' killed at Luxor?"

"We've kept good control of those activities here," Khalid reminded them. "Except for that shooting in the Hyatt lobby."

"Even we will have problems until everything is in the hands of Arabs."

And there it was again. You would be happy to wring the neck of every person he met in England, starting with those ridiculous student radicals.

"We are always first to speak out on behalf of the Palestinians. We give massive amounts of money to struggling Arab countries," Khalid said. "Not one of those countries came to our aid before oil. We need science. We need trade. We need infrastructure. We can't have any of that without peace. Peace will last longer than oil."

"Peace!" Samir exploded. "Do you know what they do? They pretend they want peace, because they need our oil. They blow up their own countrymen and make it look like us. They want to discredit Arabs, blacken our faces, and make us look like monkeys who ruin their wonderful peace. The Americans draw cartoons of our leaders with words dribbling from both corners of their mouths and beards that looks like cactus prickles." The ridicule of Arab leaders reminded him of how shunned he felt in England, how caricatured. "But that is how they are. The Israelis teach them. They send Mossad agents to work with the CID and the CIA, then set the whole thing up to look like it's Hamas. I think Hamas is a Zionist creation. I don't think there are any Arab suicide bombers. It's all Israelis masquerading as Arabs. You know all the Jews got out of the World Trade Center. It's an excuse to take our land and oil."

Khalid erupted with laughter, dismissive and paternal. He did not hear the incendiary mixture of spirituality and power that signaled the depth of the trouble your son was in or notice the angry sunset flush his face. You think how the aggressive instinct in men disables their intuition, makes winning take precedence over understanding and interaction a contest between wills. They need a code of honor just to institute civility in a dialogue that is not geared toward understanding. Anything from an alluring woman to a secular idea can distract their thoughts away from God onto conquest. You will not get help from Khalid in a battle whose existence he does not see.

You heave yourself from your perch on the bed, pace around the room, rapping your knuckles against the furniture, wondering *what* kind of group is this Gulf Jihad, *what* you can do to help your Samir. You must revive your intimacy, whatever the cost. You pick up the brochure and see the passage you've been dreading.

"Brothers, take up weapons in the service of Allah! It is time for YOU to become part of the Great Jihad! In the name of Allah and His Prophet and Messenger, God's great and wondrous blessings upon him, true believers must crush the infidel coalition who is trying to destroy the Ummah that unites all Muslims. Seventy-two virgins await the arrival of every brave *shahid* in the gardens of Paradise, for the death of every warrior for Islam, whether on a bus or a battlefield, is a cause for celebration in our world and eternal reward in the next, an honorable and glorious sacrifice in the service of Allah!

Let those fight in the way of Allah who sell the life of this world for the other. Whoso fighteth in the way of Allah, be he slain or be he victorious, on him We shall bestow a vast reward. (4:74)

> '*And fight them until persecution is no more, and religion*
> *is for Allah. (2:193)'*
> *Allahu Akbar!"*

Their cold false faith releases an obstinacy in you, the first phase of an immutable determination that has impelled you to achieve every goal you ever thought vital. You slam the pamphlet against the black metal of the stereo. The *American-made* stereo, though its cabinet is Italian and the bookcase British.

Khalid can prevent Samir from renting his own apartment until the business has taken wing. This will give you time. You can surround Samir with people whose ideas challenge his; comrades, family. It would be wise to enlist others in this cause, but you can trust no one until you know more.

Samir will come to you if he is disturbed; he will come like the little boy who carried iniquities home like deaths. You must concentrate only on him, create warm maternal openings in which he is safe to talk. If you listen carefully to his statements, position yourself as a thoughtful confidant, not a rival against whom he must pit the strength of his beliefs, you can question what he thinks is *al-haqq,* insert small alternative truths into the weak spots of his vision.

You must gather the information you need, whatever boundaries you must cross. You must battle to supply his mind with alien and fearsome weapons: freedom, curiosity, a tolerance for private and divergent opinions. You must permit him – and yourself – the intelligence of doubt. The future of your son is at stake. The future of your world.

Supermax

Jude trudged into the bar behind his uncle. It was winter and cold, night early and tar dark, wind whirling the falling snow. On the threshold, they stomped flakes off their boots, Jude unsnapping his parka, his uncle pulling off his billed hunting cap. Blue Dog was the rougher of the downtown bars that stayed open year round. Dim as a brothel, its heavy oak bar knife-scored, the Dog glowed twilight like a fire in a hearth, a place where every stray and outcast felt homey and drank long. Jude was a newspaper man, a journalist, if you could call a local heroes column in small town papers and online gigs journalism. His uncle worked security at one of those minor companies on the strip, the easy targets who got stalked as though they were big. Tale for you, Bucko'd grunted on their way down, nothing more.

The new guy had found his way into Bucko's cast of buddies less than a week earlier. His name was Mike and he was just in from Florence, where he'd worked at the Supermax. The ADX Florence was the one super-maximum security penitentiary run by the feds left in the country, and only the hard core thrived there, the kind that came from jobs at outfits like Blackwater or other mercenary corps overseas. Those guys, they vacuumed in money, if not from the job, then from the graft and the extortion and the smuggling; they were the Mafioso of the paramilitary and they were *tough*.

Bucko drank with the boys on nights he wasn't working, and he liked to take Jude with him. He slugged back beer and whiskey as hard as any of them, but he never touched it anywhere else, that was his secret. Bucko was a big man, maybe six two or three, and meaty, but his torso was long and his legs short, so he loomed into sight like a bludgeon on pegs, supersized but proportioned like a dwarf. His head was big and his features small, making it hard to tell what he was thinking, and Bucko wasn't the kind of guy anyone stared at to find out. You could smell power on him like sweat and iron.

Jude had been working in Colorado for five years by then, doing his hero columns, plus a little part-time work as a stone doctor, restoring old travertine and slate. Work like that sucked the jabber right out of his system, slowed his mind into stone cool stillness. Jude was solitary, like Bucko, though in a dreamy kind of way, because Jude was a reader. He often wondered what guys like Bucko would think of him if they knew how much he used the perceptions of writers to cull sense from the world. Unlike his uncle, who followed hard trail to hunt or fish, Jude hiked for the sheer pleasure of the views. The sight of a wildflower pushing its fragile green stalk from steep mountain granite filled him with awe that gave him a quiet kind of strength.

The bar was lightly scattered with drinkers the night Mike told his Supermax story, casual clusters, a couple or two, and one woman alone right next to the five of them, drinking and pretending to scribble in a spiral notebook.

The cell is seven feet by twelve feet. It has one four by four window, set too high to see more than a swatch of sky, maybe a rain cloud, nothing to ameliorate a sense of drifting in space. In the cell stands a desk, a stool, and a bed, each made from poured concrete. Bolted to the wall is a polished steel mirror. A thin mattress covers the bed. The toilet shuts itself off automatically when it gets blocked. A timer switches off the shower before it can flood. An electric light shines on its own. There is a cigarette lighter. A 13-inch black and white television broadcasts vetted programs. Wired or wireless communication to the outside is forbidden. For 23 hours a day, the prisoner is alone. It used to be 24.

The cell door is steel and has a port in it. Through it, guards deliver food. Through it, the prison psychiatrist offers his services, armed security by his side. Massive soundproofing blocks port conversations from being overheard. The inmates of these cells have killed or attempted to kill fellow prisoners. They have attacked or attempted to attack prison guards. They have been convicted of terrorist acts. They are the most dangerous in the nation. They are also the craziest.

The prison houses up to 490 inmates. They are all male.

One of them knows how to complain.

Amnesty International has looked into his case.

Bucko's drinking gang had savored one or two by the time Jude and he got there. Pete Mounce had a fresh draught and shot in front of him and Andy Ferguson had left four empty bottles of ale behind with his regrets. The new guy was chomping down a burger special and a long strand of grilled onion, limp and oily, hung from his lower lip when he looked up. Bucko slid a chair up beside him and Jude asked the girl in the yellow sweater if he could borrow an empty chair from her table.

Be my guest, she said, motioning with an open hand. She didn't smile when she said it and Jude figured she was content to be all alone. Hungry for herself, maybe, the way he got when he'd spent too much time in a hero's life and lost touch with his own. Her wedding ring looked like two rings soldered halfway together and she didn't wear other jewelry. Like a creek filled with spring runoff, a girl without jewelry.

I was there. I heard 'em, Mike said, after swallowing the last huge chunk of his burger. The size of the bite, the sheer mass of the bolus in his throat, said, *I'm a man's man.* A man's man was something Jude would never be, though Bucko was, and he took regular-sized bites with lots of time inbetween. Jude expected to watch the chunk bulge its way downwards, like prey through a gullet.

The girl at the next table was watching intently and Jude winked at her. She purged the interest from her face and lowered her head, but Jude could tell she was still listening. She wasn't pretty, her black hair a frizzy cloud around a face whose features were too coarse to harmonize, but she had a magnetism that pulled at him.

92

See, they put the big shot killers in their own unit, Mike said, in the brazen stunned voice that meant a first telling. That's why they ended up in the yard together.

Why the hell would they do that? You-bragging-asshole was implicit in Mounce's tone.

Because they pumped up the security just for them. Max in the Supermax. Mike chuckled, brash and edgy. They can't talk to each other in the unit; hell, they can't even see each other. They're in isolation cells. They can't hardly tell if it's day or night.

Bucko slapped a hand flat on the tabletop. The natural world was his ballast. How could anyone survive without a glimpse of it?

These guys, they're whacko. They don't kill for the reasons men kill. Not for love, not for revenge, not even for money. They aren't normal, I tell you. Mike pulled at his scrotum.

Jude felt himself snap into high alert, his bloodstream pumped with jittery champagne tension, and Bucko reacted to the change. Fill us in, he told Mike, in his marine command voice.

They used to let the Big Three exercise together. After one of those scum-loving drippin' heart groups started whinin' and hollerin' about the poor guys never seeing sunlight or havin' anyone to talk to. Like the federal max slammer should take care of their minds. Like their minds weren't horse crap before they got there.

Big Three? This was Mounce. Trying to poke a hole in Mike's story.

The Oklahoma City bomber. The World Trade Center bomber. The Unabomber.

Timothy McVeigh, Ramzi Yousef and Theodore Kaczynski together in an exercise yard, was he fucking kidding? Jude had read plenty about them, though not in their own voices, except Kaczynski, whose work was so disembodied he didn't really have a voice. Distortions of all Jude had come to see as heroic, especially proportion, especially the deep core morality that fueled the valiant impulse, they all thought of themselves as heroes. But exercising together? Talking to each other?

I was there. I saw 'em, Mike said, for the third time, his big swallow a tom beat between words.

They let them stroll 'round the yard together? Disbelief slimed into Jude's voice.

Hey, kid, you don't stroll 'round the yard in the Supermax.

Jude's his name. Bucko spoke with quiet gritty command, Bucko-ese.

Jude. Judass. Mike ever so lightly drew out the last syllable. All I'm sayin' is in the Supermax you exercise in a cage. All three of 'em in separate cages but in the yard at the same time. So's they could talk. And I heard 'em.

Jude slid into Cormac McCarthy eyes. He'd just finished reading *The Road* in which two males, a father and a son, wander through the wreckage of civilization trying to find safety, but there isn't any safety. Kaczynski would have liked it. Civilization had ended for him long before the Supermax. As he looked around, Jude realized McCarthy's vision was honed paranoia. Kaczynski eyes. Kaczynski's way of life too. Alone in the woods, everyone a potential enemy, techno-industrial development the force that finally destroys life.

The aggrieved inmate launched a million dollar suit against the U.S. Federal prison system.

The prisoner, Ramzi Yousef, *was then allowed to exercise together with McVeigh and Kaczynski, and the three men developed a bizarre friendship,* reported Simon Reeve in *The New Jackals.*

Yousef had been howling that he couldn't survive such conditions. There was no light, no exercise, no company. Yousef was smart, though not as smart as he thought he was. America's prisons were the worst in the world, he caterwauled, insinuating that he had the connections to get the word out. It wasn't true, but truth was a malleable thing, something to be used in the service of higher goals or private needs, and Yousef was a master user. Like any other raw material, and he knew explosive materials well, truth could be wrought into a powerful weapon. He would go crazy, he wrote, without other human beings to talk to. He made this claim in so many places that through sheer repetition people believed it.

Monitoring the communications was lax, a phenomenon Yousef counted on in his hurricane of complaints. His co-conspirator, Mohammad Salameh, managed to communicate with another cell of terrorists, and Salemeh had only half Yousef's wit. The man had been stupid enough to go back to the place they'd rented the yellow Ryder van that carried the truck bomb and try to get his money back so he could buy an airplane ticket home. It had taken six days to capture Salameh. It had taken two years to get Yousef.

More than one humanitarian group took up the cause. The next thing Yousef knew he was in the yard, in a cage big enough to run circuits in. Ten feet apart, a wire net above to keep the choppers from getting in, but in the yard where there was sky and air and two prisoners to talk to.

Those motherfuckers used planes to blow up the World Trade Center, Mounce sneered. Died, you know.

That was the *second* time, Bucko corrected, low and gentle. Mike here's talking about the first time. 1993. When they used a truck bomb.

Who the fuck remembers that? Mounce jerked his head at the waitress to bring him another. He wanted to hobble the lips on this Mike. Force him to stop slathering on the mustard; the man truly swaggered in his seat. Pete wasn't feeling like much of a success these days. After two bad years, he had sold his small cattle lay to one of the rich hobby ranchers, a computer mogul from the fancy part of the west; he was hired help now, a ranch hand, a saddle bum. He hated the way they did things; he hated keeping his mouth shut; he hated the bitter taste of his own saliva and the bilious color inside his eyes. And now his oldest son had been busted on a second DUI, was doing time spearing up garbage around the town's parks and public buildings, dressed in a flaming orange vest. Pete didn't want to talk about prison.

Mike pushed his chair back and it scraped across the floor loud as a retort. He unfolded his thick frame, small like a pit bull, and moseyed toward the men's room. The slow gait harvested time for him to observe everything around him, a trait Bucko liked. Bucko went way back with Pete Mounce but no history could earn his loyalty about trivial crap. If Mike's story made him a big man, that was fine with Bucko. Jude slid into Jeffrey Eugenides eyes. Eugenides would like the idea of a dialogue between terror perps. He'd slit Mike's mind like a corpse, if he thought there was a story in it.

Bucko greased the gears when Mike got back. Ironic and savvy, Bucko was as crafty as Jane Austen. Not that Jude would admit reading her, not even to the girl who'd gone down on him during the series. Of course, Jude knew what Austen had done for women 'cause she'd done it for him, made it sexy to love a smart girl.

Bucko had a neutral way about him, could make it so no one felt the burn of shame that made men do what they despised. Mind me gettin' this straight, bud, he said, sheltering Pete from his own ignorance.

Mike shrugged like he moseyed, nonchalant but alert. Jude sloughed away Austen; he needed Coetzee or DeLillo, gelid unrepentant men who liked the dark unpleasant recesses of the warped and the savage.

Bucko got Mike to go over the information Mounce needed: that during Mike's watch he had guarded the three biggest terrorists America had known before Nine-Eleven: Timothy McVeigh, who massacred One Hundred and Sixty-Eight people at the Federal Building in Oklahoma City; Theodore Kaczynski who over the course of seventeen years used letter bombs to Kill Three people and Maim Twenty-Four others; Ramzi Yousef who nearly brought down the World Trade Center in

1993, Killing Six and Injuring a Thousand more. Used a truck bomb the size of a garage! 1,200 lbs! Mike sounded disgusted, but there was something else, a furtive awe, a sly implication that this super macho feat rubbed off on he-who-knew-their-tales. Jude felt revulsion slide through him, like shit through an anus, and knew that this fecal ooze was what Pete had reacted to. The woman in the yellow sweater was also staring, her face mangled like she had just seen an auto wreck. It was an infinitely sad face, like she'd seen a lot of carnage.

Mike was the kind of man Jude usually stayed away from. The only predictable thing about him was machismo and it made him a dangerous man. Even his sense of honor would be skewed in some unjust or cruel direction. But Bucko was right; this was a story.

Timothy McVeigh was shocked when they took him to the yard. He disciplined himself with military rigor, stayed clean and wellshaven, muscular and fit, spoke respectfully to the guards, expected no mercy. He had a reason to do what he did, which in due course he thought would be honored. Someday people would know that he, Timothy McVeigh, with scant resources and assistance from just a few loyal friends, had saved America from those who wanted to destroy the fundamental freedom of the Second Amendment. Federal forces had showed their true colors at Waco and Ruby Ridge, and while many he knew deplored it, only he had been willing to risk his neck to stop it.

Guns. Powerful as the presidency, the heft of a SAW light machine gun on the shoulder. Invulnerable as a general, that's how a good weapon made him feel. He had spent his life handling guns, starting alongside the only person who'd truly loved him, his grandfather who'd taught him how to hunt. Then in the army, then Iraq, in the special forces training he'd failed (through no fault of his own), as a security guard, and finally in the gun show circuit where he'd met others who thought like he did: that you had to take down the people who opposed the right to bear arms. He was sorry about the kids, though. He hadn't meant to kill the kids.

Locked in one of the three open-air cages was a dark haired, brown skinned man, tall and skinny with huge ears and eyes like wet cannon balls. Pacing up and down in a frantic, uncontrolled way, the man looked like an Iraqi and it gave McVeigh the willies. McVeigh liked his killing distant; the sight of a dead rabbit or a bloody man could make him vomit like a coward. He could feel those swampy eyes crawl around him and fought the urge to scratch or jerk. The guards shoved him into a cage, clanged and secured the door.

The man greeted him at least six times with variations of hello, how are you, pleased to meet you. His English was accented but good. McVeigh ignored him and broke into a run. A run! Ten times around the cage, his muscles happier than they'd been in months. Then he stopped. A third man was being hauled into the yard. A skinny unkempt bugger, ugly and old. He didn't even look at the other two; he just started doing circuits in a slow jog.

Julie Brickman

The prisoner looked like a scarecrow in motion, his corpus askew like a clumsy yard bird. Sick, lame and lazy: the embodiment of the dork who never got picked for a team, scoffed alone in the mess hall, never made it through a single rough drill. Just watching his doughy flapping limbs evoked a visceral urge toward derision.

Did they become friends? Jude tumbled back into his own sensibility, trying to jigsaw a picture.

Mike cut the air with his chin, small and bullet-smooth, still streaked with onion grease.

My God. How come no one knows about this?

No reporters in the Supermax.

Oh, Christ, of course, Jude thought. He couldn't get in there, no matter how often he tried. He'd wanted to interview Woody Harrelson's father, a hit man who'd murdered a judge. He asked what they talked about.

Girls. TV.

McVeigh thought he was a super warrior, like the big ape with the forehead ridges on Star Trek, Mike cawed. Misunderstood by everyone, but really honorable. McVeigh identified with that. Wouldn't say a word against any of his buddies, even when they turned against him. And he wasn't afraid to die, I'll say that for him.

McVeigh saw himself as a patriot?

A hero. A *give me liberty or give me death* hero.

In Jude's experience, heroes came in all kinds of packages: bitter, sad, isolated, confident, happy, but one thing they had in common; they never saw themselves as heroes. Others in their situations had been heroic, but they were just ordinary folks doing what anyone would have done. What was it that let a man define himself as a hero, when he was in fact a staggeringly cruel brute? Maybe secrecy, the failure to subject one's ideas to scrutiny by the world? It took a coward to satisfy a passion so unexamined it could only be performed in the dark.

Perhaps, too, an inability to tolerate doubt; to ponder alternatives. Combined with the gutter to glory myth of our culture. Jude couldn't pin it down exactly; his nature was too full of doubt to pin anything down.

They had a terrible fight, Mike said. All three of them.

Theodore Kaczynski didn't like company. He had been content to be isolated in his Montana cabin and he was content to be isolated in his cell. He had a lot to occupy him, a country to warn, treatises to write. America was on a breakneck course to destruction, had been since the industrial revolution when men were first separated from the fruits of their work, a phenomenon accelerated now by technology. Armageddon was coming, suited up in the wardrobe of progress, and few seemed to perceive more than a wrinkle of it. Kaczynski had always been bright, so bright he thought people were trying to torture him when they asked him to describe each stepping stone he'd cobbled into the path to his conclusions. His wasn't linear thinking, it was a great web of diverse facts and ideas brought together in a burst of insight, and he couldn't help people reconstruct it, least of all though conversation. So he read, he thought, he wrote, he labored to express what he knew to be as real as a log or a

Julie Brickman

leaf. The human race was dying. Men could not survive abstracted from the land and the hunt. Of his conclusions, he was sure: his convictions were based on evidence anyone could see. Opening minds was the problem, why he'd resorted to mail bombs. He wanted to unseal people's eyes, blast away the complacency that shored up their blindness. He'd chosen targets carefully designed to represent certain issues – pollution, techno-logy, dirty sciences like genetics. Well, he couldn't use that method anymore, but he could still read, he could still write, he could still push to communicate his predictions.

But not with the two in the yard. He identified them right away; he'd followed both of their trials. The buzz-cut, clean-shaven guy with the Mr. America features was Timothy McVeigh. Stupid and hasty, his bombing. Too overwhelming for anyone to see the point behind it. The one with the squashed chin and the large nose, the pleading look in his heavy-lidded eyes, had to be the Arab from the slums of Kuwait and the wilds of Baluchistan, the truck bomber. He'd followed Yousef's trial, knew him to be an opportunist, totally without principles. Glory was what he liked, glory and making people suffer, inflicting vengeance and misery on anyone he thought had injured or humiliated him. He had no values, religious or political.

Kaczynski continued his laps. Neither of his yard mates was worth his time.

They fought? Jude asked.

Man did they, Mike said. Intense, that McVeigh. He'd rant about gear and run on about space, some TV show he and the A-rab watched. The Unabomber hated it. Thought all that geek stuff was ruining America. The A-rab, he just wanted to fuck the blond techno-babe. All the weird metal all over her hands and face made her sexier to him. I mean, he wanted to fuck every girl on the show, especially the ones in power. But McVeigh, he hated the show with the techno-babe. Voyager. Hated chicks running a military ship. Hated the captain and her cold mannish voice. Hated the chief engineer, especially 'cause she was a warrior, all fiery and strong. A warrior culture, *that* he admired. Their sense of honor; their search for a good day to die. He got the Arab to watch reruns of The Next Generation instead.

Jude didn't like calling Yousef the Arab, but he was a raptor for stories, so he went along, sliding a glance at the girl at the next table. He saw himself: revulsion and fascination, but then there was the unfathomable, incomprehensible sadness.

And you know what the A-rab said, Mike went on, sucking in the attention.

Jude knew exactly what Yousef would say, some psycho libidinous fantasy about the ship's counselor, the empath. Yousef had tried to date the court reporter during his trial, sent her a note through his lawyers asking her out for dinner, that's how crazy he was. He thought it was sexy to be a terrorist.

He said the counselor was hotter than the techno-babe. That her soft flabby heart would make her a slut to your nastiest dreams. McVeigh looked like he wanted to snuff him, then emptied his face.

That blank face, man, it meant fury. McVeigh could switch into a nutcase in a flash. Just push one of his buttons. The feds. Gun control. That man loved guns. He was like obsessed. Kaczynski, he liked guns for survival. He didn't care about machine guns. And the A-rab, man, all he wanted were mega weapons, high tech explosives, nukes if he could get em. Boy, they were three different animals. Not at all like each other. But not afraid of each other either. Wary, maybe. Sniffing each other out. Mike took one of his big swallows.

Did they think alike?

Mike's face shone across the dim table like a blue moon, and they could see the sweat on it, pearls of grime. He belched out a sound meant to be a chuckle, and it had irony in it but also shock. Jude had come to know that grunt of shock from the mirth of heroes, the ones whose feats had decimated the very roots of their beliefs. But this was what Mike had come to talk about, no doubt about it. Jude could see it in the coiled tension of his squat ropy body. Jude ordered a round.

Kaczynski claimed McVeigh's beliefs grew entirely from his obsession with guns. That he made up reasons to hate the government as an excuse to own bigger, better weapons. Said McVeigh loved guns the way real men loved teats or ass. Boy did the Arab get a laugh out of that. Spoke good English, the Arab. Had McVeigh teaching him slang.

Mike rubbed a drizzle of sweat with the back of his hand. What Kaczynski had said next was fuel for a rampage. That McVeigh was bullshitting himself if he thought he'd done any good. That he blew up the whatchacallit building for nothing.

Mullah. How did McVeigh react?

He knew Kaczynski was after him because of the techno-blonde discussion. One day, while Yousef was raving about the ways he wanted to fuck Seven of Nine, Kaczynski muttered. . oh, you'll never believe this. Mike trailed off.

Haven't up till now, Mounce muttered, his face so close to his drink, his skin looked amber.

Jude looked at the girl, and her eyes egged him on.

I'll believe you he told Mike. He was in Eugenides again. Mike didn't have the imagination to make anything up.

Mike started to snigger. A weird nutty laugh, not at all manly, more like a little boy who'd heard a fart, catchy and unstoppable and embarrassed. His eyes still looked mean, though, and Jude kept his face distant from the merriment inside. He attempted to fold respect into his expression, but he was pretty sure he failed.

Bugger Star Trek, Kaczynski spat, when Yousef and McVeigh began a discussion of yet another episode. He thought the show glorified the left liberal values that were already destroying the country.

I beg your pardon, McVeigh said.

Yousef laughed. Don't you want to fuck the Techno-babe?

Fuck her!? I want to BE her.

It just slipped out. Unfortunately, it was true. That had been Kaczynski's gut reaction when he saw her. All those years, bunkered down alone in his Montana cabin, planning and executing his strikes against the soul-destroying effects of technology, all those years living with serious manly purpose, and still when he saw a beautiful girl, he wanted to be her. He could feel the flush pounding through him and scrounged for words.

I meant, we're all going to be her, if we keep going down Tech Road. Rammed to the balls with nanoprobes or completely superfluous.

McVeigh pounced on the chance to ridicule the man who had called his life's work useless. Sissy, he jeered. Holed up in the woods to hide. Killing by proxy, one lousy mark at a time. Never a soldier, not in 'Nam. And they had the draft back then too. But you got out. Fighting in a real war wasn't for you. You're a coward. A real jacked up coward.

Kaczynski knew he was a coward, but not about that. About himself. He never had the courage to be himself. No one did. That was what the liberals had done to society. Made it impossible to be a man.

Yousef laughed again. Kill in the open, man, and you can fuck everyone. I'm a hero back home. The girls fuck me. The men admire me. The Imams laud me. The best families want me for their daughters.

Were you too crazy to be drafted? McVeigh ranted. Too faggoty? A homo? His laugh was bitter and cruel. The inside of that blank face had advanced to the surface and it was vicious. Survivalist, my ass. He skewered their bond. They ought to put you in the girls' jail.

Kaczynski was a lonely sob, Jude remembered. Skipped a grade or two as a kid, then didn't fit in with all the boys and their surging testosterone. Entered Harvard at sixteen. Probably miserable there too; all those silver-spoon blue-blood boys groomed by wealth and tutored at elite private schools, admitted into their exclusive clubs where the likes of Kaczynski never got in; some of them pretty dumb too, even if they did become senators or CEOs. Jude's father had been there, seen it all, then taken a position at a college in Maine.

Aloof, eccentric, isolative, withdrawn: those were the descriptions Jude repeatedly had read. But how did that make Kaczynski worse than any oddball? Thousands of blue collar kids went to Harvard; adolescent boys always had problems with girls, half the world had miserable families. Of course, Kaczynski had been in one of those CIA mind-control experiments designed by Harvard psychologist Henry Murray to fracture the ego. But so had a lot of others who hadn't holed themselves up in a Montana cabin and plotted to letter bomb personal targets. No, it was in graduate school at the University of Michigan that something bizarre had surfaced. Something relevant to this claim of Mike's, that Kaczynski wanted to *be* the techno babe Seven.

Kaczynski had fantasized about being a female, that was it! He'd discovered that to think about being female aroused him. He'd considered a sex change operation. Went to discuss it with a psychiatrist but didn't get past the waiting room, before shame and rage overtook him, and he bolted. It had all been in the psychiatric court report.

Mounce threw down his drink. Now I know y'aint worth a pile of dung. That's a serial killer y're talkin'about. He stalked out, slipping some dollars he couldn't afford on the waitress' tray as he went.

Jude suddenly got it. That waiting room choice had been Kaczynski's personal Armageddon: when he realized that science had the technology to give him what he wanted, but he didn't have the courage to go for it; when he knew he could have a sex change, but chose not to. After his refusal, when he'd fled from his yearnings – fled from the shame of them – his desire warped into hatred of the very things that could satisfy it: technology, science, and social change. Kaczynski's hits had been pointed: a geneticist, two computer geeks, a public relations executive defending Exxon after the Valdez spill (the same firm representing Blackwater now). By the time he secluded himself in Montana to live life as a survivalist, a man as he thought men should be, his desire had been thoroughly warped and buried: subterranean but hum-ming away at the core. His brilliant mind was fettered, its only aim to create theories to inter the humiliating failed desire.

Jude felt a figure loom out of the dark, beside his chair. He looked up to see the girl in the yellow sweater. Her face was hard, the mangled look shadowy underneath.

Girls' jail, she said. A real party, the girls' jail. She laid a hand on the back of his chair and waited for the attention she knew would come. Bucko swiveled his seat with an obvious grinding sound and put down his ale. Jude felt his heart go off in his chest, like a round of buckshot. He thought he would always see her standing there, that sad, mangled look, the weighty legs planted, the yellow sweater, the blue spiral journal. Do you know who was in the women's supermax? she said softly.

She had to know none of them knew or cared, but she was going to say her piece. It might have been the first act of courage Jude had actually witnessed. Ordinary courage; the kind he was trying so hard to comprehend.

A girl who never killed anyone. Not a mass murderer, not a serial killer, not a terrorist, not a mobster killing by proxy outside, not even a slayer of inmates. Just a woman who refused to testify. In a maximum security slammer because she wouldn't lie about a real estate deal. Wouldn't give a federal prosecutor the President or the First Lady's head on a platter.

Not that you care, she said, and left. It was a quiet leaving, a few soft strides of her running shoes, a stir of air. The only thing that lingered was the fresh, sharp, surprisingly floral scent of her perfume.

Iggies

The other week, I received a notice from Facebook indicating I had been invited to a newly formed group entitled Writers Who Have Set Work in the Remote Recesses of the Chinese Uighur Region.

The invitation had come from one of many writers I had Friended on Facebook but didn't actually know. She was, I discovered, a member of many such groups, including Writers Who Can Only Find the Truth While Naked, Writers Who Have Received Over Five Thousand Rejection Slips (in which I found I had 101 Mutual Friends, though, happily, mostly writers who publish in *Martha Stewart Weddings*, the *American Rifleman* and *The Weekly Standard*) and Writers Who Secretly Think They Are Better Than Anyone on the *New York Times* Best Seller List with subgroups variously entitled Openly Think; Better Than Anyone Who Has Won the Pulitzer; and Better Than Anyone Except Virginia Woolf.

This made me curious about what has been happening in the writers world since it had copulated so fervidly with the Social Media World in the forms of Facebook, Twitter, Google Plus, and the growing new sites of Grumblr (no 'e'), In Your Face, and Google Minus All Those Tech Dummies Who Still Use Facebook.

I didn't suspect anything nefarious at that point, mind you, though I probably should have when I followed the click trail of an extremely popular post (3,896 Likes beside the Raised Thumb) that led me to a website (with a downloadable app) entitled Best American Stories, Essays, Poems & Books Written by Writers with Small Vocabularies aka Iggies.

Using the backup California toll browser, Bandlock – California being the first state to generate crog (a word derived from crash and smog that indicates the presence of a radioactive state generated from simultaneous use of wireless devices in a given region) and therefore having developed specialized browsers to address stoppages on the Internet Superhighways. There is also a Free Browser called SigAlertOnLine which reroutes you through a less utilized area, slowing down the speed of your connection by a factor you can find by multiplying the number of wireless devices in your town by the number of moun-tains and high rise buildings (added together) and then adding in the number of stars visible on a clear night, preferably in winter, from your rooftop.

SigAlert, for those of you not from California, is a system developed by a Los Angeles broadcast executive named Loyd C Sigmon to let motorists know where traf-fic has come to a dead halt for 30 minutes or more for no discernible reason. There are approximately 71 SigAlerts on an ordinary commuter day and 129.5 during rubber-neck or tourist season, which in LA, comprises the entire year minus the religious holidays of Christmas, Ramadan and the new quasi-religious International Buddhist Self-Immolation to Free Tibet Day For Those Who Are Not Afraid to Come Back as a Dog.

It turned out that the number of Writers Groups online had expanded beyond the scope of my imagination on a bountiful day. These went by monikers that I decided to catalog for my new interactive web blog and downloadable app site catchily named Find a New York Publisher for Your Book Here, with links to the Lower 49, lower indicating an artistic rather than a geographic calibration.

The first group had a sidebar of favorite links, irresistibly titled things like Writers Who Like to Talk About Their Work More Than They Like to Do It; Writers Who Compose Their Best Sentences While Unable to Get Them Down Because They Are in Their Cars; and the sad Unfriended voice of a Writer who had translated Molly Bloom's soliloquy into the linguistic patterns of Elmore Leonard and was looking for others interested into making High Art accessible.

While I was categorizing, preparing for my IAO (Initial Amazon Offering) of Scaffold Your Platform: The Writers' Guide to Influence on the Social Media, which, to my surprise an augury of agents seemed to want, I ran into an interesting phenomenon. There was a whole branch of groups strictly for MFA students. Fortunately, resurrecting my identity as a Vermont College alum, I penetrated their rather flimsy firewall.

The first group that caught my eye was called Writing Students Who Think They Have More Talent Than All of Their Mentors, with its myriad of variations including Expect to Win Major Literary Awards, Expect to Attain Immortality Through Art, and my personal favorite MFA Students Who Submit Their Grandmother's (Crap) Stories Under a Cantankerous Mentor's Name.

There was also a Submission Slut website whose simple registration process allowed writers to gangbang submissions out to every current contest with a single click. There I discovered that *Narrative* has started to offer the most innovative of its contest-rich, fee-laden career – the zero word story contest. The first winner was of course Ernest Hemingway who has lately produced zero word stories with surprising regularity. William Faulkner, it seems, was incapable of producing zero word stories, despite his entry into the state known as Permanent Writers' Block, unless of course his stories were produced by a member of the Submit Your Work Under the Name of a Famous Writer and See If it Gets Accepted group.

Not to be outdone, *Glimmer Train*, had launched a Minus Ten Word story contest, in which readers, for a Plus Ten Dollar Fee, could enter as many times as they wanted. Rumor has it that a mathematician, quite capable of all kinds of negative communication, has won the first contest, in spite of a great deal of competition from a fast growing neo-Rushdian group called Writers Who Have Never Guillotined a Good Line aka The Putter-Inners Writers Group aka Narcissyphus.

By now, I had spent close to 313 hours on Facebook and Google Plus and Minus, not counting browser time on Chrome and Dogpatch, and a new icon was stalking me, interposing itself between me and the text, with an irritating rolling sequence of antiquated writing tools like typewriters and paper and bookshelves.

And there it was again. Best Iggies. In I clicked. Iggies it turned out was short for ignorant. Of course at first I thought it was a spoof, a list of authors whose vocabulary was smaller than that of a bonobo or the border collie trained by its owner to understand a thousand words. A list of authors who put guns on the page and never shot them or forgot who slept with whom between the covers. But no, that wasn't it either. Ignorance was not a pejorative, it was a Movement. It had downloadable slogans. Literacy is an Entitlement. Civil Society (bleeding heart icon) Censorship. Cure Culture. It had links to authors: Tom Clancy, Ann Coulter, David Mamet, Tom Wolfe. It had a picture of Vladimir Nabokov reading the *National Review.*

It turned out that all these writers clubs were arms of a single Facebook sponsor whose identity took me hacking lessons to find. For a mere twenty-five dollar registration on my new Hacks, Hackers & Geniuses Interactive Website and Blog, you can purchase this verified, true piece of information, a priceless commodity in the Age of Factual Enhancement. With it, free of charge, you will receive a copy of the new authorless text The Art of Ignorance (for the Hopelessly Intelligent), a delightful compendium of random excerpts from campaign speeches, filibusters, tweets, and Internet customer reviews. Alternately, by downloading my newly developed Liester/Cheatster Software you can discover thousands of brilliant passages to lift from works that have run out of copyright.

An Old Arabian Folk Tale

In the old days, in a village called Qaryih in a remote corner of the province of Ubar there lived a young man and a young woman who were deeply in love. They were ordinary people, though blessed with intelligence, strength and health. Extraordinary, however, was their love and from it blew breezes of happiness. People liked to draw near them, to catch lightness from the spirits that gathered around them.

One day, the man said, "I love you with all my heart, but I have not seen much of the world. What if there's a place finer than our village? What if there's a woman more perfect for me? I have to know."

The woman had no such feelings, but she was not willing to discourage the fire in her lover's heart. "Go and seek the experience you crave," she said.

"When I return I will tell you everything," he pledged, his hand pressed to his heart. "Will you wait for me?"

"Know that I love you more than anything else on the face of the earth or the realm of the sky," she replied. "Know that our love is enough for me."

Salman packed his belongings in a knapsack and started down the path from his village. Curiosity drove him forth, though his heart yearned for Yasmine. On the first night, as he reclined near a stream, a sleek fish, pursued by a predator, arced out of the water and flopped beside him. Observing the fish, Salman saw silvery grace rather than food, submerged it in a flask of water so the stranded fugitive could rest peacefully through the night. In the morning, before gliding into the water, the fish thanked him and said, Save the water I slept in until you need clarity. May God's blessings be on you.

From dawn to twilight for nearly a fortnight, Salman trudged until he crossed the peak of Jabal al-Akhdar and spied a village in the valley. Longing for company, he arrived at the doorstep of a cottage where a woman of allure and charisma beckoned. Inside, the cottage was a library; walls of books lined every room. Even the bathtub was arranged for reading. A paradise for the intellect, Salman thought. Nothing like the mundane cottage Yasmine had furnished, those dull mealtimes of chatter about nothing.

The woman (Mona) made Salman feel brilliant. She asked questions that probed and expanded his thinking, waited until he asked to hear her ideas before she took a turn. They talked until sunrise, his mind racing.

Day and night, they debated all the great ideas of the world. He loved every parry, hungered to expose himself to ideas he hadn't examined. Not one thing did he say that Mona didn't elaborate or hone and he found himself doing the same. Then a strange thing happened. His thoughts about life started to deplete. His intellectual dexterity faded. A drone: the bore one dreaded at parties, that's what he became. He reached for the fishwater and sipped until clarity brought the resolution to flee. Desire to see ideas in action burned inside him.

Salman slipped away from the hamlet of intellect, remembering how Yasmine had never challenged his ideas, never made him feel scant of wit or a fool. Intellect alone was a desert, he reasoned. Perhaps kindness was the key, a woman who would soothe rather than stir him.

He rambled a long ways through the low country and during siesta settled near another river. Listening to the water's sweet babble, he fell into a pleasant slumber. While he dozed, a coterie of river maidens gathered in the lapping currents. On their tailfinnies, they slip-slopped down the soggy riverbank until they'd scooped out a giant slide, down which they pushed Salman, into the river, where they floated him on a raft of their satiny swimming bodies.

He woke on a riverbank, feeling as though he'd been rocked through the night in a cradle of water. Under a nearby tree, whose arcaded branches bore flowers petaled like butterfly wings, a hidden path led to a cottage. On a sunlit verandah, weaving, sat a beautiful woman, a garland of butterfly-wings encircling her hair.

The river maids' song foretold you would come soon, she cooed, and invited him in.

She fed him soup like nectar of silk and warmth seeped through him like a sunbaked afternoon. Between sheets softer than the oiled skin of a concubine, Salman dreamed his body floated on a carpet of clouds, while beside him this handmaiden rubbed every inch of his skin with lotions from flowers and the oil of butterfly wings. To ruffle such tranquility felt brutal or vulgar; to make love like raping a butterfly. And Salman cherished the peace; it was exactly what he wanted.

Salman considered himself a man of mighty will, but soothed by the maiden's balms and herbs, there was no need for will. Squabbling was a thing of the past, conversation superfluous when every wish was anticipated; it was serene, this home. One night as Salman reclined in bed without a yen in the world, he remembered his pledge to tell Yasmine whether he was sure of their love or had found someone better. A thread of discontent ruffled his mind and he tiptoed to the other bed to observe the woman with the halo of petals. In place of her silken face lay a statue of marble, as ideal as those sculpted in ancient times. God help me, he exclaimed, I have fallen in love with a piece of stone.

At the sound of his cry, the statue awakened and gazed up at him, her empty sockets filling with the eyes he knew. You have discovered my secret, she cried. Serenity between two requires the suppression of one. By satisfying your whims before you feel them, I create absolute tranquility, and you have no need for disappointment or desire or ambition or passion (or adventure, he thought).

But without you, I have no life in me. As she spoke, her marble skin acquired translucence. The crimps in her stone hair separated into shimmering strands of platinum. A floral aroma from the circlet of petals seeped into the air, perfuming it for the new day.

If he waited until this goddess, this nymph, became fully herself, they would resume their idyll, so similar to death. Salman rushed from the cottage and with a rattle it crumbled behind him.

Gazing upwards from the valley where he stood beside the rushing river, Salman detected some kind of village or fortress that looked like it grew straight out of the rocky peaks. So natural, so like the granite of the mountain, were the buildings that the ramparts looked as if they had been thrust upward by Nature herself. Salman filled his flagon with fresh river water and hurried along the dusty path up the mountain. At the gate, a sentry barred his entrance. Your papers? she asked.

I am a traveler. I seek the finest woman in the world.

Ahlayn, dear Salman. We have awaited your arrival a very long time. You seek our Queen, Aminah bint Aminah. The sentry seated Salman on a camelback sofa in a room shuttered by windows and departed.

Immediately, in pranced three guards wearing red dress regalia fringed with gold. Their job was to undress him.

A cocky little guard pointed to a golden circle shining down from a domed skylight in the roof. Stand there, she ordered. The cone of pure light exposed every inch of his shucked body.

When Salman was an infant, his female relatives had greeted him by kissing his penis in homage to its ability to bestow life. So small, so weak, so deficient in firmness, yet so important: his penis. Inside, Salman carried this feeling, this sense that he possessed something worthy. When stroked, he felt himself teem with life.

A brawny guard placed a meaty hand on him, pulling not with awe, but with intention.

Take its resting measure first, the squat one snarled.

The third guard, thin as a falcon feather, ambled slowly around him, inspecting, making notes. Salman felt himself wither. Was his penis important or not? Unrolling a slender tape measure, the brawny guard extended it flush along his penis and tossed her head like a snorting horse, braying, I don't know why all the fuss about this one.

He's the One. The irritable runt spoke like she was in charge.

They measured every inch of him: limbs, chest, buttocks, toes. They even took photographs, though never of his face. In the end, they handed him papers, which catalogued, among other things, his sexual characteristics. Erect his penis measured 17.5 cm., flaccid 10.2. Identity papers: he was required to carry them any time he appeared on the streets. Having passed this examination, Salman qualified to go on to the next stage. Queen Aminah bint Aminah, they assured him, would be worth the trials.

In Lashiba, clearings were gardens; streets meandered like paths. Vivid but unfamiliar flowers spilled along walls and trellises, balconies and gateways. The mountain-peak village was beautiful and tranquil.

It took a while before Salman noticed anyone on the streets, for pedestrians granted him space. No one bumped into his energy much less his flesh. Even a rendezvous of eyes required a small ritual of exchange before it occurred. Staring seemed almost a violent offense.

Salman was used to making small gestures of aggression to assert his mettle over anyone on his path; he didn't know how to walk without swagger. To stay distant from others he was accustomed to invading, if only by a hair, threw his gait out of balance; the invisible circumferences compelled him to dodge shadows. If someone else's physical presence wasn't a challenge, how was he to act? He felt awkward as an ape, an inflation of himself. Even his fingers were too large.

There was something strange about a village where intimacy did not require one will overriding another. Salman wasn't sure he liked it. Who could be satisfied without ascendance?

In a clap of awareness, the source of the strangeness revealed itself. Everyone on the streets was female! His machismo ascended as if bathed in ice. No wonder there was so little of interest. Where were the men?

Everything that had seemed graceful looked ugly. The flower arrangements were sentimental, the patches of garden tidy, domesticated. Vistas receded into neat pastoral landscapes, their wildness illusory. Considerate gestures seemed fatuous compared to the grandeur of aggression, the postures of hierarchy and competition and war. A lifetime in a place envisioned by women was surely the definition of Hell. Nothing of consequence could happen here. He had to leave.

Then he remembered Aminah bint Aminah. It was said she was a perfect woman, the very purpose of his quest. A man was measured by the women in his life. Driven by the ambition he saw as curiosity, Salman had to meet the Queen of Perfection.

Aminah bint Aminah was radiant, mythic. Her figure was luscious, her eyes luminous, her hair raven and waterfall-thick. When she summoned Salman to her chambers, she was scented with wind, swathed in raiment spun from heaven's light. In spite of being a ruler, she was intelligent and humorous, flush with a ribald sense of life. How Salman blessed his good fortune.

In between his nights with her, too few by far, he entertained other maidens sent by her, lovely young things who satisfied his lust for a night then disappeared forever. Never did he see any of them a second time.

One day, ambling through the city, he came upon a secret garden. Interspersed with the greenery were abstract sculptures, each named and dated, as if they were human figures. Aminah told him they were sculptures of the spirits of persons who had died or departed, Lashibans' way of memorializing their dead. You could actually recognize the ones you knew.

Horrified, Salman recognized in a Medusa-limbed figure the young girl who had come to his private chambers the night before. Was it her, he demanded. Aminah laughed: No no, we don't murder them, she said. We have no violence here. She chose to die for the good of the community, for she knew she had become a carrier of evil and would awaken feelings like jealousy or competition. A contagion of decay ensues when an individual places her own good ahead of the common good and she did not wish to cause an epidemic.

Does everyone who comes to me die then? Salman asked.

It depends on the feelings they notice in themselves or in others around them. We monitor feelings very carefully. We understand their power to create or destroy civilizations.

Salman was now aware that his touch initiated a march towards death. The next time a girl arrived in his chambers, a candle that burned flames of darkness flickered shadows across the floodlight of his desire. The following day Aminah told him that a girl who came to him had not elected to die.

For days, constrained lust collected dark fires within him and he searched the city for other sculpture gardens. No one in Lashiba died from infections or fevers, as they had in his home village. Illness, Aminah told him, had simply disappeared as they learned to eliminate envy and rage, anxiety, cruelty, hatred and contempt. Long before blight could decay into disease, citizens willed themselves to death.

So consummate was Aminah's ease that the discomfort of a single cell would draw the focus of her formidable mind. When they were together she was entirely with him, so deeply that he heard a singing within him and understood sexuality as the greatest of all arts.

Yet the darkness in his interior grew. Aminah would not give herself unless she was in a perfect mood, so he made love to the damsels she sent and then sought their memorials in the concealed gardens. No other monuments ever appeared. Death occurred only by election and birth, almost as rare, sparked a celebration across the village while each resident decided what she would contribute to the raising of a new Lashiban. Long life was the ideal here, for everyone it seemed but the martyrs.

At the fringe of the city, Salman discovered another cemetery of sculptures. Here the perverted form he had seen was multiplied a thousandfold, as though limbs and torsos had been arranged in a deliberate violation of every aesthetic sense. Who were these awful people?

They are your predecessors, Aminah said, other out-siders who have come to live with us; to get their snort of paradise before their dark and perverse interiors caused them to die in an agony of resistance and fury.

But surely many of them had chosen the examined life of the seeker? Surely, having found their way here, they merited better?

Solo exploration is a narrow and limited path, Aminah replied. The wellbeing of every cell is also the wellbeing of your own. Do you know that if one of us falls, another may develop the bruise?

The idea of an event in one body causing a conse-quence in another, in many others, ramified as he consi-dered it. There were so few men here, yet the women were sensual, playful, the way women get when showered with male attention. And then there was Aminah's sexual concentration; so powerful. He hesitated, stammered, when we make love, do the others . . . ?

Aminah smiled. We never know who will get pregnant.

All of you? Everyone in the city?

No no no. In only some of us have these abilities come to fruition. The others still have failings, still contain imbalances of individuality or negativity. From them, I select a maiden to send you, for they must slowly be eliminated.

Aminah's perfection was the culmination of an evolutionary process; what Salman had sought around the globe, and yet he felt horrified. You must go now, she said. Your lack of empathy could start an epidemic in Lashiba.

Salman had been with every woman who had walked or strode or sidled through his dreams and each of them was flawed beyond repair. Now only Yasmine haunted his dreams, Yasmine and home.

Through thicket and forest, mountain and escarpment, dune and wadi, Salman wandered towards home. Finally, he arrived in his village. No one recognized him as he crossed into the village square. At the gate of Yasmine's cottage, he hesitated and hid behind the gnarled trunk of an ancient tree. What if she was married? What if she no longer wanted him?

Yasmine came out to the garden. Sadness hung around her mouth, adding depth to her exquisite beauty, and he knew she still missed him. He opened the gate.

She recognized him and stood in stillness. He flung himself on his knees in front of her, clasped her hand in his, told her that nowhere in the world existed a woman as beautiful, as intelligent, as enchanting, as she. For sure, he could love no other. He asked Yasmine to marry him.

"Oh no," she said. "I cannot."

"You do not love me?"

"I will always love you."

"You love another?"

"Never another."

"But I am certain. There is no one better than you."

"I was never interested in certainty."

"What, then, do you want?"

"What you can never give."

"To you, I will give anything."

"I wanted you to take the chance."

Gear of a Marriage

Year One

1. Hiking boots, 2 pair, 1 Lowe's Superfeet 6 ½ ; 1 Vasque Skywalk 10 ½ .
2. *Afoot and Afield in San Diego County*; *San Bernardino Mountain Trails*; Idyllwild Rental Cabins & Hiking Trails.
3. 1 Tempur-pedic classic king bed.
4. 8 Tvilum-Scanbirk 84-inch cherry adjustable-shelf bookcases.
5. 2 Herman Miller Aeron chairs.
6. 1 four-wheel drive Honda CRV, electric blue.
7. 1 used BMW 530-i, white with tan interior.
8. *Wild France: A Traveler's Guide*; *City Walks, Paris*; *Larousse Dictionaire du Vocabulaire Essentiel.*
9. 1 set All-Clad stainless steel cookware.
10. 1 Starbucks Barista Aroma 8-cup thermal coffeemaker.
11. 1 Braun PowerMax blender with replacement blade.
12. 1 cane.

Year Two

13. 1 Multi-Pure Drinking Water Systems reverse osmosis filter.
14. 2 Kenmore Progressive air purifiers with HEPA filters.
15. 1 Breville Fountain Elite juicer.
16. 1 Kitchen Aid 12-cup food processor.
17. 2 molded leg braces.
18. 1 set Table-Mate adjustable height TV trays.
19. 2 dozen boxes Simply Thick nectar-consistency thickening gel, pre-measured packets.
20. 1 Braun Thermoscan ear thermometer.
21. 2 Legget & Platt S-Cape adjustable electric twin beds.
22. 1 Landice Rehabilitation treadmill with 0.0 starting speed, reverse gear, and safety locking system.
23. 1 Lifeline CarePartner Communicator with personal help button wrist monitor.
24. 1 Pari reusable nebulizer with angled mouthpiece and tubing.
25. 1 molded torso brace.
26. 1 adjustable commode with safety grip bars.
27. 3 Evolution walkers, black.
28. *Caregivers Guide.*

Year Three

29. 1 travel and transport wheelchair.
30. 1 Bipap bilevel positive airway pressure breathing apparatus with external humidifier.
31. 1 Fisher & Paykel Opus nasal pillow mask.
32. 1 mechanical insufflator-exsufflator Cough Assist machine.
33. 1 Pronto power wheelchair, borrowed.
34. 2 Bruno vertical platform wheelchair lifts.
35. 1 Pressalit Care electric adjustable sink bracket with lever control, 1 wash basin with gooseneck faucet and blade handles.
36. 2 plastic urinals.
37. 1 handheld shower with glide bar and 5-foot hose.
38. 1 Sunrise Medical DeVilbliss portable suction machine.
39. 6 Yankauer suction tubes regular capacity, sterile.
40. 1 Permobil K/C300 modular power wheelchair with removable headrest, pelvic positioning belt, joystick, tilt and recline adjustment, seat lift, emergency signal lights, and rear caregiver controls.
41. 1 ergonomic computer table, wheelchair accessible, cherry.
42. 1 Toyota rampvan with E-Z Lok system, leased.
43. *Functioning When Your Mobility Is Affected.*

Year Four

44. 1 Pulmonetics Systems LTV 950 portable volume ventilator on assist control mode.
45. 1 Resmed Ultra Mirage full face mask with adjustable headgear.
46. 1 Masimo pulse oximeter.
47. 1 free-standing medical trapeze bar.
48. 1 Panasonic Toughbook augmented speech computer with Stephen Hawking E Z keys XP software by Words Plus.
49. 1 feeding tube, size 16 French.
50. 4 60-ml. syringes for bolus feedings.
51. *Adjusting to Swallowing and Speaking Difficulties; Adjusting to Breathing Changes.*

Year Five

52. 1 hospital bed.
53. 1 Spillproof urinal for supine use.
54. 1 Cyberlink brain-actuated computer input and navigation system.
55. 1 Invacare Micro Air alternating pressure, low air loss mattress.
56. 1 Hoyer electric hoist.
57. 1 eye-gaze activated wheelchair joystick.
58. 1 Respironics 22 mm sip'n'puff angled mouthpiece for 24/7 vent-dependent usage.
59. 1 advance health care directive; 1 durable power of attorney.
60. 1 adult Ambubag single patient use resuscitator.
61. *Palliative Care in Amyotrophic Lateral Sclerosis.*
62. 1 urn.

Breakfast on the Balcony

My neighbor is sitting on the balcony, getting fed. His tee shirt, a cheap turquoise affair, is rolled up to expose a swimmer's torso and clipped by a clothespin near his neck. The turquoise matches the startling color of his eyes, which cut across the canyon to gaze at the ocean and never once rest on me.

A clear plastic tube flops out of the middle of his abdomen, hanging as flaccid as my husband when I tell him I want to get pregnant. Nat and I have been married eighteen months now and he hasn't spent a piker's dollar on the house. Next door they've done two renovations, if you count the one to handicap.

I ran into the wife at the bank the other day. "Livia, Liv," I called, smiling a big smile, not really something I felt inside. A frown braided her brows, like she didn't know who I was. "Sheridan," I said.

Focus hardened her eyes and, crumpling the bank chit, she banged her hip against the trashcan.

"Great stairway," she rallied, referring to the railroad ties we'd had Mexican laborers embed in the slope between our houses.

"It's the rope lighting," I told her. Tracing the stairs down the side of the slope, tiny lights glow like a necklace of expensive jewels.

"Lovely," she said. "Now the burglars won't trip on a dark night."

A New York transplant, she has that sarcastic wit no one out here in the West likes. I think she sounds Jewish like my husband.

"Seriously, they look like starlight, your stairs." Then, like she read my mind, she said, "How're you and Nat managing the religion thing?"

Tears jumped to my eyes. I don't know if it was her sympathy or the subject. She steered me by the elbow to the bench, her grip hard as uncut stone. There we sat, two neighbors who barely speak, gabbing in a parking lot behind a bank.

"He won't have kids with me unless I convert," I found myself saying.

"Well, you can only be absolutely certain who the mother is, that's the Jewish point of view." Then I swear she said, "Like Mary," though I was crying so hard it only hit me later.

I told her I barely got through design school, how could he expect me to learn a language like Hebrew. He doesn't want to spend the money. Kids are expensive.

"It's not important to be right," she said. "It's important to get what you want."

She picked up her purse. It's pumpkin orange, like a fall leaf, the only bright thing about her. "The fertile season passes very quickly," she added, rising.

Livia's husband is a handsome man: six feet tall, skin robust for a blond, Christian for sure. He's morbidly lean, I realize, refocusing on her balcony, his legs thin as twigs, his arms caving in where biceps should bulge. Next to him, a squat muscular man, brown as a Mexican, has reappeared on the balcony, carrying a red Coke can. He pinches off the abdominal tube, suctions the brown liquid into a thick syringe, positions the tip in the valve end of the tube. For a minute, it looks like he can't get the plunger to move, but then slowly the blue tip inches down the cylinder. Suddenly, the end of the syringe pops backwards and liquid spurts like a fountain. The husband lets out a shriek of rage and fear, coyote-loud. *That's* the brown stain, I think stupidly, because the man's flailing like he's been struck by shrapnel. The caregiver wraps his strong hands around the man's tumbling body, cooing Shane, Shane. I don't know if the husband is going to get aligned safely in his wheelchair or slam hard against the Trex flooring. And I think of the conversations I've had with Livia, how I've never once asked what's wrong with her husband, what that tube is in the middle of his stomach, or why he can't speak anymore, and, as I wonder what kind of person she must think I am, I realize I've never seen a neighbor enter her house with a grocery bag or a foil-covered platter and I know if I have a baby that's how it will be for me, because in this beautiful beach town neighbors are strangers not friends, and sadness overtakes me but I have no idea what to make of it and I wait for it to pass.

The Rainbow Range

Muhammad kicked the kinks out of his leg and reached for a cigarette. Everyone in the jeep sat puppet still, even after he'd climbed out. They knew he was dangerous from the way he'd hurtled the jeep down the steep side of the dune, relishing their terror. Stealthy as cats, the five passengers slid from the jeep, paced and prowled nearby. Muhammad ignored them as he ignored the flies that spiraled around us, the only stir in the feverish desert air. I took the cigarette he offered, bent to the flame cupped in his palm.

"Where are we?" I asked. We were surrounded by dunes as tall as the one we'd plunged down.

"In the Rainbow Range," Muhammad said. "Look."

A halo of pale pinks, mauves, corals, amethysts, and the yellowest topaz colored the dunes and the light around them. The dissonant glint of a strange color, blue as sapphire yet mottled to lapis in the shade, flashed like flecks in an opal. Standing on a floor of gold as yellow as twenty-four carat, ringed by the glitter of bejeweled dunes, I felt as if I'd entered a Shahrazade palace.

"Mother of God," I said. "Why doesn't everyone come?"

"Quicksand," Muhammad replied. "Very few can tell where it is."

No one could identify quicksand according to the British explorer who'd charted these sands, but then he was not from desert stock, neither Arab nor Badu, and Muhammad was all three. "Shall we set up camp? Muhammad asked.

"Samir has the heaviest equipment." Samir was the other driver in our two-jeep caravan across the perilous desert the Bedouin called The Empty Quarter, my business partner in this East-West amalgam of adventure travel.

At the mention of Samir, my bearing grew unconsciously affectionate and Muhammad stepped into its warmth. "He'll be here," he said.

To strand a friend in the desert violated a code of honor I knew the two men shared, and yet the plaintive sound of the honk honk I'd heard before Samir and his jeepful of tourists faded from the side view mirror echoed in my ears.

We set up what equipment there was, which included the big dining tent, stripped of its luxurious rugs and cushions, a latrine shelter, and materials to build a fire. Muhammad knew what he was doing, but did things alone. When we had to cooperate, the negotiation about method took longer than the job. Tension with a flirty edge thickened between us. I kept glancing into the distance for a cloud of dust, hoping Samir and the others would arrive before the scenario went too far, for I did not trust Muhammad and flirted only to palliate the danger he posed.

Knotted near the jeep, people's conversation sounded skittish and tense. A random mix of nationalities and backgrounds, my half of the tour group had jumbled together a British expatriate couple who'd lived all over the Middle East, an Egyptian academic who had written an infamous book about the brothelization of life in Arabia yet covered her head to show her allegiance to Islamic values, an American political scientist whose mother was a Holocaust survivor, and Nell Houston, who'd never hiked past her own backyard but had filled a set of hand-blown glass beads with the seven colors of the desert sands.

"I miss the green already," Nell had muttered to me on the flight. She had gazed across her husband's bulky form out the porthole at the deep desert where we now were to camp.

I stared at the glittering palette of burnt colors, the dizzy swirl of unfamiliar desert forms, and mused, "I feel like I might spy a bizarre color, a bronzed sapphire, say, or a silvery melon."

Nell gave me a funny look, her small face, under the halo of frizzy red wisps, porcelain-doll pert, even when daunted. Her husband had been vaulted into an executive position by his Texas oil company employers; a Middle East position paid sky-high wages these days because of the risk. Nell improvised a gay little laugh which changed to tears before she managed to ask, "What're you doing, honey, going to the end of the earth?"

"Snatching the job opportunity of a lifetime," I'd told her, though it didn't feel that way tonight.

Muhammad pounded the tent stakes as if he could drive his aims into the group's prattle, then tried to bark them into calm. Fearful of an incident, his temper became my primary concern. If it hadn't, perhaps I would have noticed what was happening in time to prevent it.

The travelers had gathered in the shade of the big awning, wanting the comfort of nearness. The light had been changing for a while and its influence altered the mood of the group. An affinity seeped through them, an alliance. In the succor of attachment, each one of them grew more distinctive. The light seemed to generate the difference, as if its odd pastel radiance empowered this mélange of accidental nomads. We sat peacefully in this semi-meditative state, our communication easy yet honest. A few people sipped drinks, though the effects of alcohol seemed subdued. The wind ruffled around the dunes, carrying odd, distorted sounds on its currents. Once, it seemed to call my name. Emma, implored the wind. Ehhmmaa. An eerie, distorted faraway sound. A while later, it keened again. This time it no longer sounded supernatural. I scanned around to see if anyone else had heard it. Muhammad's ear was cocked to the wind. I caught his eye and we both listened. Ehhmmaa. It was real, alright. Someone was calling me.

At first I thought, someone from Samir's group was calling from the other side of the dunes. Then I realized, Nell was gone.

People had been coming and going, disappearing into their tents or to relieve themselves. Nell had left, when? when? I pulled up a picture: Nell leaving in light the color of pale honey; nearly two hours earlier. Sunset was just now beginning, the sun's sphere tumescing as it began its long descent towards the rim of the sky. Quietly, I checked Nell's tent but she wasn't there. Nor was the equipment she used to gather sand for the miniature crystals she filled to make necklaces.

Of course! I thought. Nell's gone to collect the blue sapphire sand. Nell had no idea how unforgiving the terrain was, how the sameness of the landmarks befuddled the senses. It looked so simple out there, friendly as a sandy beach. And then, there was the quicksand.

Muhammad was waiting outside the tent. He had done a quick survey of the rest of the camp and found no sign of her.

"What will we tell them?" I said.

"Tell them that no one is to go out there alone, ever." He instructed me to wait while he retrieved some equipment from his tent. "Such stupidity offends the law of the desert," he muttered, as he disappeared.

Of course every member of the group volunteered to come, but only someone with Muhammad's expertise could track in the desert. "We need a contingency plan." The English expatriate spoke in a tone quiet enough to convey enough urgency that he didn't have to say, in case you don't come back.

He proposed himself as contingency driver and his wife as navigator; both of them had extensive desert experience and fair enough skills, but they needed a location and a route. Muhammad had changed into an odd pair of shoes, slung a pack over his shoulder, and returned to the fringe of the group. He slipped forward when I beckoned and stood beside me, scanning the expedition map I'd spread out on the camp table. On the map, our location was not far off course, though in an area Samir had explicitly planned to avoid. Muhammad zigzagged a finger along a circuit and explained how to get around the tall dunes and back to the known byways. At least four of the group memorized every word.

Before we left, I drew the political scientist aside. His suspicion of Muhammad had been palpable during the trip and I thought he might have the knowledge or connections to understand what was at stake without explanations. Sure enough, he had a satellite phone of his own. He had, he assured me, plenty of contacts he could raise.

Muhammad was pacing around the edge of the encampment, studying the sand for signs of Nell's footsteps, like an antediluvian tracker from the era of silk and opium. I scrutinized the mountains. None of the dunes was particularly distant; a novice could hike to them without difficulty. Nell would not have attempted it otherwise; she wasn't courageous. But that blue sapphire sand would have magnetized her by its exquisite beauty, overridden any dread. A saddlebacked dune to the west looked as if an alpine pool had spilled pendulously from its edges, a frozen sandfall of blue gems. Nell would have beelined for it. I called to Muhammad. "I think she'd have gone that way." Surprise cast a shadow across his face. He had just identified tracks that led in the same direction.

We set off, me trailing slightly behind to avoid kicking sand over the faint marks he was tracking, though I felt certain that unless denser veins of color marbled another dune, we needed only to head for the blue sapphire fall. "What's in the pack?" I asked. Mine contained a skeletal assortment of gear: microchip compass, army knife, headband lantern, flares, trail food, water pouch, microfiber sleeping bag, jacket, but his bulged with equipment. Rescue gear, he explained: a coil of rope to pitch to Nell if she needed it, a sand anchor, titanium stakes whose tips flared into hooks, emergency blanket, extra water. He also had this large apparatus that looked like a scuba tank with a pump arm. It turned out to be an instrument devised to spew a stream of heavy sand into the pockets of space in quicksand, to firm it into a hanging sand bar and create a temporary bridge, which, like logs on water, would eventually drift away and disintegrate.

Why was this visionary piece of equipment not listed in any of the gear catalogues, I said, intrigued but skeptical too; all those hours of searching. His family had developed it from a system used by some of their ancestors, he explained. Slinging rocks with precision could force a stream of sand into an area where a man or a camel had become stuck, so they could scramble to safety.

"It had no use except in the deep desert," he said. "It is like the Badu."

Human beings had walked on the moon; the Americans and the Russians had staffed an outpost in space; microchip technology had engineered instant communication, yet the Poles and the desert remained unconquered. I said as much to Muhammad.

He looked at me. "The place conquers the man," he said.

There was an illusion wilderness expeditions evoked that hard travel made participants rugged and invincible. I asked him to explain.

"The land calls us. It sings to us. And we must go."

"The desert is stronger than the man," I murmured.

"This is what happened to Nell," he said. "She was not prepared for its seductiveness. She could not say no."

Periodically, Muhammad inserted markers into the sand, colorful iridescent flags attached to what looked like titanium poles, inflated like bulbs at the base, that seemed to float half-immersed in the sand like buoys. When one of them refused to stabilize, he turned to me, "She doesn't seem worth this much risk," he said. I assumed it was because she was American, an infidel, bilking the geyser train, but when I asked, he said it had been Bedouin custom to calculate risk versus gain. Three of us could die to her one.

The blue dune grew more radiant in the waning light. Sand lapped over our feet and filled our shoes, lacerating the skin and making each step heavy. The dune was further than it looked and the distance seemed to elongate as we walked, yet the sand's radiance drew us like a physical force, the siren call of the desert. Sand from Muhammad's boots spilled back onto the desert; they were vented with tiny chutes that reversed the influx, another family invention probably, certainly a piece of gear unavailable in the commercial market.

The wind had ceased its eerie moaning chatter. No longer did it carry my name, elongated into a spectral aria; in its place was silence, a voluminous black sound as dense as night.

Suddenly Muhammad stopped and cupped his hand over his ear. "Listen," he mouthed. "Listen."

I cocked my ear to the wind, but shook my head. He moved towards me, his hands curved into a trumpet, which he placed gently over my ear and tilted in the direction of the blue mountain. A faint human sound of crying became audible.

Muhammad moved swiftly. The desert was his terrain and he knew how to cross it. Like a gazelle or an oryx, he was fleet and at home, and it made him beautiful. Stumbling along behind, I said, "Go without me. Go." He turned, his jaw set in silent refusal, and sprang towards me, removed the pack from my back, and tossed it into the sand. Beside it, he dropped a turquoise marker. "She's not far." He snatched my hand. "She'll trust anything you tell her to do."

He guided me along, until I almost skimmed along the top of the sand. It was as if he could change his center of gravity, move it upwards to lighten his weight on the sand and create spin from the force of the earth's pull, an inner levitational wave that enhanced his momentum and flexibility. Centuries of evolution had gone into that motion, I thought, as I watched him bound along like a featherweight cat. At the foot of the dune, he squinted in concentration, pinched samples of sand between his fingertips. "From here on up, it's treacherous," he said. "You wait and listen. I'll call to you when I need you to speak."

I could hear the crying without assistance now. It was a broken, discontinuous sound. "I'm coming," I said.

"The sand will never bear both of us. You have to stay. Keep the end of this rope in your hand, so you can guide me back, if I need. Keep a light on."

In the North, I could have insisted but this was not my terrain. Though it would have been foolish to go, I was surprised how sad it made me. I asked what to do.

"I'll either be able to rescue her or I won't. If I'm not back in an hour, return without me. The markers will guide your way. Do not, under any circumstances, try to find me or Nell on your own. Do not deviate from the markers. Understood?"

I nodded.

"You will be able to hear every sound either one of us makes. Do only what I tell you. Do nothing else, even if she begs you."

My eyebrows made their own little dunes. Surely, if Nell wanted encouragement, if hearing my voice could provide strength or comfort, I would give it to her.

"Even the sound of your voice can interfere with what I may need to do. The very pitch of the sand can give me a crude sense of its density and pull."

I raised my hands in surrender. "I promise, I promise." But was it true, what he said?

He was deft, yet slow, careful to examine the sand with each step as he climbed. Quicksand was just sand in motion, vibrating and colliding at high velocities. In most places, it was no more than a few feet deep and by letting your body float and paddling, anyone could escape. But quicksand was odd here, unpredictable. A rainfall from years earlier could have oozed to great depth or an aquifer reserve seeped gradually upwards. According to lore, currents of wind could create this fluxing effect, tremors of earth. Quicksand here could be deep enough to drown someone, especially if they panicked and flailed, as Nell probably had.

Muhammad had to traverse the trough between dunes, where at any moment the sand might not support his weight. His buoyant gait seemed to positively toss him from the ground, as if he could walk on air or water. The crying sound had started again and it was mixed with mumbling, like a toddler giving herself courage when no parent was nearby. Hold on! I wanted to call, we're here, but I pictured the sound of my voice making Nell struggle and sink deeper. Muhammad had disappeared around the circumference of the dune. The light from the last rays of the sun wavered like a guttering candle. I waited for the cry of Muhammad's instructions, grateful we had found Nell before it was too late.

A crack of thunder reverberated through the air, as loud as a gunshot. What a horrible time for a desert downpour! The sand would get slick, the quicksand would worsen, the trail markers would be knocked off their pins, hypothermia would endanger the exhausted Nell: everything would quadruple in difficulty. Worse yet, a sandstorm could blow up, a gloomy winter *quwas* or a southwesterly *suwahillih*. I gazed balefully at the darkening night sky. The dim sparkle of an early planet pulsed near the horizon, the stars still ghostly augurs of brilliance to come, but I could see no signs of a storm. There was no storm. It must have been a gunshot.

The crying sounds had ceased. I strained and strained and strained, but could hear nothing. She doesn't seem worth this much risk.

The flies would ravage Nell. They swarmed over anything here. She would sink into the sand, her head upturned, flies all over her face, feasting on the moisture of her eyes, darting into her nasal passages, her open mouth, onto her gums, her palate; turning all her orifices black and maggoty. They would swarm the wound too, swill the ambrosia of her blood. Nell Houston: the innocent of the group; the babe. Were the rest of us condemned too? Had I made some horrible mistake by coming here, meandered as naively as Nell into a lethal struggle I couldn't understand?

The soft fall of sand mooshed, Muhammad returning more quickly than he had gone. He materialized beside me, his final approach as silent as annihilation. Sapphire sand flecked the rope hanging from his belt.

"It's okay," he said. "She's alive." He reached out to steady my trembling arm, but stopped inches away, his hand hovering like a drugged moth. "She was stuck but the quicksand wasn't very deep. It was not difficult to pull her out, but I couldn't bring her all the way back. She needs food, water, a little rest. Then we can take her back to camp. She'll be able to walk with support."

"Thank God," I said. Thank god, thank god, thank god. I looked into the enigma of his eyes. "And thank you."

"We must go to her," he said. "Seeing you will give her strength."

Nell was just around the flank of the dune. A single track of footsteps, already receding into ridges and hollows, wound upwards. Muhammad must have carried her down.

Nell wept when she saw me, a hoarse sound like the cough of an alley cat, but Muhammad cautioned her not to talk. I dropped to my knees and wrapped her in my arms, cooing, stroking her hair, then took the supplies Muhammad handed me and spooned protein drink down her mouth, hydrated her with electrolyzed water from a nipple bottle. Color seeped into the scared whiteness of her face and dappled the blue on her lips.

Supporting Nell between us, we started to trudge back. Muhammad beamed the flashlight to and fro in a wide hypnotic arc. I paused at a marker, but Muhammad shrugged no and I decided to leave them as artifacts that might endure beyond our scraps of mortality. Nell mumbled something unclear and then lapsed back into a half-coma, unable to apprehend a word we said.

I watched Muhammad buttress Nell's weakness with strength and delicacy. I examined his small-featured profile, the meaty lips, the vague stretch of chin under the beard he seemed to have grown since our first meeting at the ranch. This was the face of a terrorist? A man willing to execute innocents for a cause? He could easily have killed either of us or made us hostage to his cause. The only witnesses in the desert were the lizards and the flies.

"If you could not have rescued her, would you have . . . her?" I made a garroting motion across my throat.

"In quicksand, suffocation is slow. It is without mercy."

"So why fire the gun?"

"She needed adrenaline." He pushed his face around Nell's body to make it clear he'd registered my mistrust.

"That is the real desert," he said. "When it's stripped of your visitor's romance."

A dome of blackness thickened the night around us. Masses of stars like distant torches lit the way. On the far horizon, the glow from a bonfire released a column of smoke like a signal: come home weary travelers.

"You would not have questioned me, if I weren't Arab," Muhammad's tone was ruminative as much as accusing. "And Muslim."

"I wouldn't have doubted Samir," I contradicted. But I might have wondered just a little. Nell made a small whimpering sound.

The half-quadrangle of tents was no more than a few hundred yards away. A supersized fire shot flames of yellow and orange into the sky, conquering the blackness and warming the cold. Compared to the desolation of the dunes, it looked like civilization.

Muhammad must have heard me mutter for he waved a hand around him. "Imagine the cities that were once here. Imagine buildings dyed in the colors of the sand, blue sapphire and gold, saffrons and cinnamons, colors that stir reverence like firelight and sunsets. Imagine rivers like the Tigris and the Euphrates running all through the land, their banks luxuriant with trees. Flowers everywhere. Eden was once in the Rub al-Khali; it's what we dream of when we die."

Lust's End

Rob scarcely noticed his first imaginal failure. A gorgeous long-legged blonde walked into his classroom and he could not picture her naked. Overtired, he thought to himself, remembering his rather inventive performance with Christine the night before. Pristine Christine, he used to call her. Not anymore.

The second incident alarmed him because he was out with the woman. Johanna Stephen Sands was a brunette with pale skin and large undulating breasts. New to academe, she was actually enthusiastic about a contract job with the English department, and she was smart: smart without the poisonous edge Rob hated in so many of his snake-tongued colleagues. Toasting kir against martini, wine against wine, they drank to her success. As he gazed through the black silk of her blouse at her creamy, plump breasts, a red circle materialized around one breast, then the other, followed by a thick red line right across the nipples. Maybe, he thought, she was wearing some new type of bra that they sold in feminist boutiques. An anti-male bra, with a little switchblade that popped out when you touched it without asking. Rob blinked vigorously several times. The red circles disappeared. He did not invite Johanna back to his condominium that night.

The following weekend at Café des Copains, a lanky miniskirted waitress strode up to Rob's table and instead of picturing her legs hooked over his shoulders, he saw them in baggy gray sweats as she jogged effortlessly past him in the park, tossing a glorious smile his way as she went. Never in his life could he remember adding clothes onto a woman. At his club the next day his imagination changed a tightmuscled young redhead out of iridescent dancercise tights into a pinstriped suit. As he watched the swing of her briefcase recede, Rob began to wonder what was happening to him.

The worst was in the classroom. This year his graduate seminar was almost all women, which he used to love. He would take them out in little hordes for coffee, and as their eyes clung to his witty, moving lips, he disrobed them. He didn't do it on purpose; an item of clothing would just slip off after he'd made a particularly clever remark, as if Henry Miller were dispensing rewards. The taut boyish woman with prepubescent breasts would suddenly look naked from the waist up; the fleshy one with engulfing thighs would ripple from a gauzy white caftan. It was fantasy heaven, his own personal *Playboy*. His tongue sprang new muscles; his brain turned new corners; his wit knew no bounds. He loved them all.

A few years earlier when the repressive university regime tinkered with its admission standards to encourage applications from women and minorities, Rob had been a vocal supporter. He had chaired the departmental committee on the educationally disadvantaged and published brilliant articles in the faculty newsletter and the *CAUT Bulletin*. When the associate dean of arts, a woman, lost the competition for dean to an outside male applicant, he wrote a scathing letter to the *New York*

Times. He acquired an enviable reputation as one of the rare male allies of feminist causes. Women poured into his classes, all types of women: old, young, black, yellow, red, pink, and coffeeskinned; women with Afros, burgundy streaks, spikes, and crewcuts, even one with a shaved head like Sinead, the Irish singer he had seen on one of those late night rock videos (in his mind, with her shaved pubes, she looked like an eight-year old girl – impish, impudent, innocent – as she stood naked before him; watching her made him tremble). Keeping up with these women took large chunks of his energy; he found less and less private time to work and think.

There had always been troublemakers, the raging dykey women who didn't think any man could be an ally. When they first appeared in his classes, he could pick them out. They were the ones in Birkenstocks and thick socks or combat boots. Devoid of makeup with straggly hair, they read Rita Mae Brown, Mary Wollstonecraft, and Radclyffe Hall. (The thought of their naked flesh repelled him; it would be reptilian, crusty and damp, with slimy intestinal pudenda.) When he made a joke about how censorship would affect the modern erotic female, they stared at him with cold, contemptuous faces. After such a class, Rob would seek the company of a gentler female colleague or student who would console him, explaining that these were separatists who believed that women should remove themselves from all male influence for a while. He shouldn't mind, they told him, it wasn't personal. But Rob was sensitive to what other people thought; those critical faces *felt* personal. He began to guide his virile tongue by their reactions.

After a while, he could no longer tell who they were. Criticism could come from anywhere. Radical voices spoke from beautiful faces. They could no longer be attributed to the fat, the old, the ugly, the unmarried. Soon they started to contradict each other in class, and it became harder to tailor his opinions to appease them. No matter what he said, some woman always found chauvinist implications. He felt like he was dodging fastballs all the time, and watched his influence dwindle as he let their voices take over his classes. One of his colleagues got hauled down to the sexual harassment center for sleeping with a student who claimed she had acquiesced only out of fear for her grade. In the men's room his colleague whispered: she was willing, she agreed, she hung around after class, spent hours having intimate chats with me in the faculty club. No one believed him. The student had spiral notebooks filled with evidence of her attempts to refuse him; she had tapes of his phone calls; copies of his letters and lists of other students who had witnessed his pathetic approaches. The colleague was put on temporary suspension and required to seek professional help. Rob's nervousness increased; things were veering out of control.

He wrote to his friend Livia, in California, who'd once been a psychologist, to ask how to handle it. "Be yourself," she replied. "If you wait long enough, women will be back in stilettos, thinking motherhood is the career path of meaning."

In classes, his favorite female students slipped further from his lusty imagination. Brenda's tight mauve sweater turned into army fatigues after he joked about Barbara Bush (less). A helmet popped onto Kim's shimmering hair when he mentioned a seminal paper. As he presented the thrust of an argument, the whole array of moist, dripping lips thinned into dry sneers. Rob hurried out of class to escape their clamoring voices, but the throng pursued him, carrying bayonets where purses once had hung.

The voices began to talk at him from inside his head: commenting, nagging, scolding, informing, judging. Doris Lessing is not humorless, pigbrain, a low voice rumbled when he stopped reading *The Golden Notebook*. Rape is the Vietnam of female experience, another chided when he flung down his fifth paper on rape in twentieth century American literature. Abortion law is a permanent War Measures Act! This one screamed at him all the way through his attempt to read Henderson's bill on fathers' rights. My body, my body, my body, she shrieked. NOT Henderson's body, not daddy's body, NOT MY BABY'S BODY, and not part of the body of law. Rob couldn't think. Pregnant women carried men's babies. That's why men picked wives so much more carefully than mistresses. He smiled: it felt good to hear his own thoughts.

It didn't last. Casting his mind around women writers, trying to find some that he liked (to not look sexist) and could assign to his classes (without stimulating those hideous domestic issue papers), he found himself wallowing around in the sex lives of women writers. Maybe this was the best criterion, he thought, to save himself from the tightcunted writing of the dyke brigade. Woolf, his favorite (the only woman he thought could write at all) had a celibate *marriage*. Rob shuddered (one day without sex left him raging). Willa Cather was a dyke. Gertrude Stein. Adrienne Rich, and who knew how many others. Then there were the spinsters: Austen, Dickinson, Pym, Sarton, Brontë (Emily). What about Djuna Barnes? Dyke? She wrote about them, implying that profound sexiness and dykiness sprung from the same vaginal wells. A weird thought. What did that mean? Independence, a voice answered; fuck a hundred or don't fuck at all, but never get stuck in servitude.

Rob hated these thoughts. He didn't want to understand the complex plights of women. Understanding crippled his aggressive tongue and compromised his ability to castrate his adversaries with one verbal swath. He no longer enlivened faculty meetings with sexy quips and irreverent jabs. The wreathe of laughter that had always enveloped his lonely, fragile soul disappeared. Once one of the voices used his tongue to lecture a colleague about the necessity of malebashing. After that, he shut his lips firmly at meetings. His big, fleshy face acquired a pinched look; his wide lips pursed in a permanent pout.

Johanna confided more deeply in him. "I want to get into tenure stream right away," she said over Benedictine and coffee. "There's a position coming up in my area next year and I'm going to apply for it." Being an academic had been her dream from childhood; her mother, a high school French teacher and a frustrated intellectual, was redeemed by Johanna's career. Professionally, Johanna used her mother's unmarried name, and with each publication, the maternal face that had dimmed her childhood with gloom, lightened and eased. Rob, a member of the powerful tenure and promotions committee, understood that he could help Johanna. He knew exactly what she should do: where to publish, how many papers, which committees to join, which to avoid. Sleeping with Johanna would ruin her; she'd just be another woman fucking up her chances. How should he talk to her then? Rob often counseled new male colleagues; he recognized their bellyup deference to his position and rewarded them with his assistance. But bellyup for women had always been sexual: what if it wasn't? What if Johanna just wanted help? Friendship? What if her intense excitement wasn't laced with sexual innuendo? Was about work? Ideas? Disoriented, Rob played safe, gave her information, and took her straight home.

Relationships fascinated Rob now. He puzzled and pondered and speculated about them, even sought women just to talk about them. He read writers he had previously disdained: Marge Piercy, Alice Walker, Toni Morrison, Robin Morgan, even resorted to social scientists like Phyllis Chesler, Judith Herman, and Ann Jones. Men in their books were vague, shadowy figures with dim interior lives or selfish, critical, violent, furious bastards. The real lives of women occurred in the spaces between their ties with men, the time the spent with each other. Men's accomplishments, their thinking, hardly mattered. Instead, how much housework they did, the type of time they spent with their children, if they were supportive (listened to women complain), dependent (had to be looked after) or possessive (undercut women's friends, passions), were the qualities of note. Incredibly, these women laughed with each other about men's sexual frenzies, how men raced around to fuck away their anxieties with insipid baby cunts. An equation appeared: strong cunts inspire weak cocks. Men, it seemed, lost their erections with strong women. They had to be coaxed, teased, coddled and sucked, which could take hours and still result in a semisoft prick. (Female psychiatrists labeled the phenomenon *Primary male flaccidity*, and debated whether it was a sexual dysfunction or an intractable characterological disorder.) Pricks, according to these writers, only stayed hard when men called the sexual shots (like when to stick in in). Some women considered a soft prick a compliment, an ode to their independence. Were dominance and hard pricks really related? Rob thought about his prick history. He'd only been impotent with his ex-wife, and her bitchiness had caused it. *Hadn't it?*

Microscopic details about male bodies littered the pages. Pectoral size, chest hair, moles, callouses, skin textures, baldness, paunches and salty smells leapt into Rob's sexual consciousness. How did he fare, he wondered, was he attractive enough? He angled for opinions from women friends and extorted compliments from lovers. When he shopped for clothes, which he did with increasing frequency, he thought about what they'd said. It became harder to decide what to buy. Christine liked him trendy; Johanna preferred the corporate look; Kim directed him to L. L. Bean. Rob bought all three and varied them according to who he might see.

Some days he couldn't manage. He didn't want to be stripped, judged, assessed, and criticized by women. He examined himself minutely in the mirror, pouring over every blemish, agonizing over every flaw. His midriff bulge, thick ears, purple appendectomy scar and flabby biceps panicked him. He loathed his body. Clothes became armor to distract penetrating female eyes.

It might be a relief to get married. To settle down with one voice, one set of eyes, and one set of opinions. But ambitious women, reluctant to endure the tumultuous clashes of will that marriage seemed to inspire, preferred lovers. "Men come and go," Christine told him, "but my flute is here to stay." Rob didn't want to settle for a witless blonde with a pallid billboard face; he would forever be propping her up just to feel safe himself, but what choice did he have. It was a woman's world. Dread invaded his solitude until he could hardly work at all.

After their next dinner, Johanna invited him back to her condo. *Maybe she's the one. She's capable and ambitious. I could encourage her; she's unsure of herself.* He whipped the cream for their Irish coffees, then carried the empty mugs back to the kitchen and rinsed them carefully. Good husband material, she'd think, someone who could look after things while she battled for tenure. Her bedroom was frilly and pink; the sheets on the delicate bed had roses on them. Rob climbed awkwardly into bed like a flabby, clumsy giant. No matter how she stroked him, he couldn't get an erection. Even when she sucked him for what seemed like hours (but was fifteen minutes by the hot pink hands on her bedside clock), he never got completely hard. Of course she asked what was wrong, if there was anything he particularly wanted her to do. Hold me, he implored, let's just cuddle.

In desperation, Rob decided to write about his condition. But his mind was severed from the genital power that had inspired his greatest work. He no longer believed in that power; it had no place in the world. Even with the help of the complete *Oxford*, not a word came.

The Back of Her

Livia soars above the steep curves of the desert canyon, then speeds straight into the windowpane of her own house and plummets headfirst into the mud. Broken-winged, dazed, coated in feelings of filth, in her usual awakening state, she hauls her granite-limbed, unbirdlike body out of bed, does sun salutation, pushups, situps, showers, reads email, checks to see how her time is. It's quarter to nine. A sliver of minutes remains before Gabriela the caregiver arrives to look after her husband. Now it's a race: can she get coffee and breakfast and get back down to her office before she has to engage with Gabriela? She's almost done, just cutting up the fruit for breakfast when in struts Gabi. "I'm going home for the night tonight, right?" she says. "We're starting the new schedule, right?"

Livia doesn't have any objection to this really, yet she's furious. She just wants to cut up her fucking fruit and drink her fucking coffee in peace. "I thought we were waiting until we trained the new caregiver," she says. Inside, she's wondering why the fuck she's saying this.

Predictably, Gabi starts arguing. You promised. You said. We agreed. What's wrong with you?! Livia has provoked this she knows, dumped the residue of her birddream on Gabi, yet listening to her carry on is enraging. "Get the fuck out of my kitchen," Liv shrieks.

Shock crosses Gabi's face and she's momentarily speechless. Somewhere deep, Livia is pleased.

Realizing she's been trumped, cornered, blindsided, Gabi storms to the front door. "I'm going," she shouts. "I'm going like you said." The engine of her red truck revs and she speeds away.

Livia eats her fruit and drinks her coffee in peace. The sweet solitude of a quiet house sings its calm, beautiful song. It's going to be a dog of a day but it's hers.

The day is hell but Livia takes satisfaction in it. Gabi, she knows, expects her to call and beg her to come back but Livia doesn't want Gabi to come back. Livia is fucking sick of Gabi's endless pushing: pushing for more time off, pushing to arrive later, pushing to go home earlier, pushing about what's best to do for Livia's husband, treating Livia's house as if it's a facility for Gabi's patient and Livia is the intruder. She is sick of seeing the counters used for medicines, of the laundry used for Gabi's personal wash, of the exercise equipment used for Gabi's workouts, of Gabi lecturing her how she should do everything from feeding her pet to treating her own husband. She is sick of listening to Gabi's harebrained schemes for how to treat Shane as if they have even a speck of merit. She is sick of Gabi haranguing her in her own home. Livia likes the image of the back of Gabi.

Livia works all day, ten am to midnight, helping her 58-year old husband, who's had amyotrophic lateral sclerosis for six years. She has not done this in months and has to study the task list she's prepared to train caregivers, go over the medications and supplements meticulously. Using the hoist on her own for the first time, she scoops up her six-foot husband by the back and legs to raise him to a seated position on the side of his alternating pressure mattress. This is after she's taken him off the ventilator, helped him urinate in the supine urinal, given him morning coffee, ibuprofen and Baclofen through his feeding tube, supplied a hot washcloth for his face, suctioned his secretions, changed his wool night sox to compression hose, slipped his underwear and pants around his ankles, put on his shoes, raised the blinds; after she's brought the recharged hoist battery from the garage, and rolled the wheelchair into position.

Now she wheels over the standing hoist, wraps the sling around him, positions his feet, presses the controls to raise him, holding his knees open. Then with him hanging midair, she pivots the hoist in a half-turn, puts Calmoseptine lotion on his butt where he's prone to a bedsore, pulls up his underwear and pants, and lowers him into the wheelchair. Then on with his tee shirt, first the head, then the left arm, then the right. Then the same with his sweater. A clean bib for the drool. More suctioning. Help him upstairs by pressing the button on the platform lift, which he can no longer do. Operate the cough assist: five inhales to stretch his lungs, five exhales to clear his gullet. Take his oximeter reading. Make his breakfast drink while he tilts – at least a half hour of opening dry capsules, pricking liquid ones, crushing tablets, measuring powders, blending in whipping cream. Then she feeds him one-handed through the syringe into his tube. Cleans it all up. Helps him in the bathroom. Tries to grab some lunch for herself.

Meanwhile, he rings for things he needs: suction, urinate again. Second feeding. Pegs down on the wheelchair. Up again to urinate (5 x today); down otherwise. Window open, window closed. Gear masks to wash. By the time he's ready for his afternoon spell on the vent, it's almost five in the afternoon. Livia collapses for an hour then makes her own dinner. Takes him off the vent. Third feeding. Gets ready for dinner and an hour of TV together. Afterwards, another hot washcloth. The reverse of the morning as she hoists him into bed. Positions the mask for venting overnight.

She falls into bed at midnight, exhausted but pleased with herself. She did it; she managed the whole routine. She had a whole day alone with her husband, private and sheltered, sustenance for a while. We were a married couple again, she thought. I could touch his flesh with tenderness, and he could be tender with his eyes. It was a rose garden in the desert, a butterfly in winter, a moon path on the night sea. The castle of their love fortified everything and she has lived there again for a day, a hard day, a grueling day, but a day she had her Shane back.

She lies back on the pillow. She'll soar for real tonight.

The Lonely Priest

Standing at the altar, accompanying himself on the guitar as he led a favorite hymn for the congregation, sparse in March when the river was still frozen and the sun shed barely six hours of light a day, Father Eugenio Laxa fell in love.

Father Gino had never been in love. It drew him into its spell like a magnet, sapping the silvery wing of his tongue as he stood helplessly at the pulpit, staring into the fifth pew, where the long-boned face of a stranger, leaning forward to frame itself between the parishioners ahead, entranced him, blanking out everything in his mind, including his homily, his to-do list, his awareness of the tragedies in his parish, until how he got through the rest of Mass he didn't know, his mind working on its own, a miracle perhaps (certainly outside natural law), while at the same time, in the terrifying swell of silence, a few of his more alert parishioners surely noticed the peculiar way he held the Bible like a shield alongside his groin (protected only by his customary jeans and sweater), as he stepped, stumbled really, toward the side podium, where, as he stared from the platform, the impossible rose to his heart, the reverberating shock that there might be something that could alleviate the loneliness of his life, the bottomless solitude of someone who had sworn eternal faithfulness to an entity who never talked back, an entity without flesh, without warm human skin, without yearning and desire, for though Gino loved the Savior and the priesthood and had learned to satisfy the gap in his being by reckless one-night stands with the consenting boys of summer, the college boys who came up to Dawson to work a few months, then after their wild, midnight-sun romp in the Arctic, went thousands of miles Outside, back home, taking with them the memory of their daring little tryst with a priest to replay in later days when their pubes were bald, their marriages sexless and their taste for men forgotten; now, as he stood speechless, riveted by an ascetic face, the eyes river brown like breakup waters silted by mountain runoff, the nose long and brutal, flat as a club at the tip; a face dark yet alert, hair black as jackboots, the gaze comfortable yet studious, as though viewing the whole chaotic mess of him, accepting all he was and ever had been; in that one cosmic moment whose significance packed into it as much as the events of an entire year, Father Eugenio Laxa understood that nothing in his life would ever be the same.

The stranger was the town's new doctor. Already the Father had heard gossip about him. Raised in a tiny conservative hamlet in Eastern Ontario, not far from the town immortalized by Alice Munro, the doctor had seized the chance to live in the in the community of his choice, the beautiful remote city of Dawson, 220 miles south of the Arctic circle, surrounded by mile after heady mile of gorgeous wilderness: salmon clogging the rivers in summer, bears lining the riverbanks to dip their great paws into the cool runoff waters, bighorn on the bluffs, caribou roaming the tundra, fox and lynx and moose, snow buntings and ptarmigan. The doctor was overqualified, a graduate of the finest schools; there was no doubt he could fill the post, though if he were fleeing something, like so many who came to the North, he wouldn't last. Father Gino regarded the tough, eager face thrust between the necks of the two parishioners ahead of him, and thought, nope, this one knew exactly what he wanted. Rumor said the doctor had first attended the Anglicans, St. Mary's rival for the hearts and moneys of the white Christian population, which meant he was probably looking to establish himself more than to worship; fine with Father Laxa, for it was a competition he always won, his love of showmanship giving him a charisma that the Anglican pastor lacked, enhancing an intimacy of delivery sparked by the isolation of the North, where he was far from the surveilling eyes of the all-powerful Church.

The Father's big voice sundered the silence. "Doubt!" Slow and harsh today, his baritone rang like the call of a moose in the snow-hushed bush. "Do you think you alone there in your pew are the only one who feels it?

"Not so. Every priest I know goes through periods where he doubts the existence of God. Doubts the stories of Christ and his disciples. Doubts the Bishop, the Pope, his own fitness to serve. Crises of faith, we call them. Tests."

Father Gino softened his voice to low and confidential, but there was a quaver in it, and it felt like a betrayal, his own insides welling up to expose him. He'd written his homily to put behind him one disaster and now a second was churning his emotions into roiling and raw.

"Many of you know that last year, almost a year to this day, my foster son, Zeke, hanged himself from a rafter in the sacristy. It was a cruel death, his soul leaking slowly from its container. A day that created a crisis of doubt in my heart and my mind."

The doctor inched his beaky face further between the parishioners in front of him and his river eyes had the fire of sunlight in them.

A blizzard of body parts, groins and testicles, sweet open butts raised high in the air, clotted Father Gino's mind, the devil risen in him as it hadn't for months: all of them looked like Zeke, though once or twice the face of the stranger sat on the frail shoulders.

The Bishop had agreed to do a funeral Mass and they buried Zeke in consecrated ground, though many days passed when Father Gino wished they hadn't, when he didn't want to see etched into the stone the meager years, 1994 – 2007, of Zeke's stay on earth or remember the tensions between them. Protection of the Church had motivated the Bishop, the sanction against suicides having been eased, but before his decision, while the slime of rumors ran thick, the Bishop had warned Father Gino: not one slaver of scandal do I want to hear ooze out of your parish again. If that happens, not even I can save you, not even our distance from the Vatican. Thank God the Bishop was an adventurer himself, a bush pilot, a gambler, and a drinker, sexually active as well, though with women.

The nurse said something sotto voce and the doctor winced, but his torso stayed still. Small towns like Dawson coddled their rumors; in the subzero weather north of sixty, tall tales warmed people, kept them company through the long dark nights when loneliness slept in their beds, laying its cold corpselike form between them and any human body. Pedophile, they'd whispered about Father Gino. It was not the truth, but he had to be careful.

Stepping down to walk through the congregation, resolve flowed through him. Flesh-driven, capricious, and mercurial in so many spheres, when it came to the priesthood, his lone ballast in an unstable world, Father Gino's mind was a fierce haven. He wanted the mesmerizing stranger with the melodramatic face, but he couldn't afford the risk.

This is Henry Brandon. The words came from the nurse's mouth but, the way they hung between the two of them, they might just as well have come from God (or his subterranean partner). *Peace be to you.* There was a clash between the priest's silvery blue eyes and the wide planes of his face, and he could see Henry Brandon noticing it, assessing the mixture of his heritage, his father Filipino, his mother Irish. He withdrew his eyes from the greeting, turning them the grey of icy footprints, and forced out a big charming smile as he moved on to welcome a parishioner in the next pew, the writer in residence, Livia Skyer. One of many non-Catholics who came to his church, Livia was the only Jew, and Father Gino ran his hand down her arm to comfort her for the rhetoric against Jews was rising as Easter approached. *This is Henry Brandon* was taking in his every move. *Fuck you*, thought the Father, pumping up his resolve to ignore the attraction, *I rule here, this is my domain.* An odd friendship

Julie Brickman

had developed between the priest and the writer, each of them taking suppressed journeys in the other's company. They laughed a lot and she laughed now, a little snort that acknowledged the inane flirtation of his gesture, together with the silly pretense of her attending mass. Henry Brandon did not look one whit fooled.

St. Mary's Catholic Church in Dawson City, Yukon was an old but spruced up wooden structure located at the crossroads of two of the eight avenues and eleven streets that formed the main grid of the town; dirt roads hardened by permafrost that would buckle any material as flimsy as concrete or asphalt. The church was a beautiful edifice, its high peaked roof and bell tower painted a pale buttery cream and trimmed in green, the rectory beside it reversing the two hues. Inside, its creamy walls dropped down to meet a wine red carpet beneath rich dark pews, and the wide arch of its chancel framed a statue of Jesus, bloodied limbs nailed to a large cross. The spare luxuriance, harking back to the days when the church was the nexus of community life, suited the church's scruffy self-reliant flock, representing what was inviolable and strong. In a territory larger than the state of California, inhabited by fewer than 35,000 people, in a town of 1800 permanent residents, hundreds of miles north of a capital around the same latitude as Anchorage, the parishioners still looked to their priest to shine lightness into that dark chill winter, where November of the soul spanned September to May.

Things happened in a town so remote the light of winter danced green and orange in the night sky, things that wouldn't occur in other regions. The North cut down boundaries, made eccentrics out of ordinary people, community out of strangers. It wasn't that the North attracted misfits; it created them. It pushed people to the outer fringes of who they were.

Gino watched Livia Skyer stir milk into his coffee, a strong bitter dark roast she bought at the River West Cafe on the street across from the Yukon River. Seated on a lumpy vinyl chair, patched with duct tape, at the Formica table in the kitchen of the Berton House writer-in-residence retreat, Gino stared hard out the window where the entire town sloped down toward the river. On the far side rolled bush all the way to Alaska.

"Defrocked," he muttered. "Such an ugly word."

"Not to me," she said, "though it seems archaic. To take off the frock. Women wear frocks."

Gino laughed, and it crept close to genuine. "Guess what vow it doesn't release?"

A voracious storyteller, Gino once had come over right after he'd overseen the digging of a new grave. "There was already a body in it," he'd confided, showing off a little because Livia loved priest stories. The body had been an old one, the bones brittle and crusted. The only way he'd known had been by the skull, its jaw and teeth intact. Probably a murder, he'd concluded; no coffin. Catholics didn't like to share graves, though by now, given all those centuries of bodies interred in small hallowed graveyards, he didn't think anyone's bones lay alone. He'd removed the old bones to make way for the new.

"Chastity," he said. "I'd have to get a special dispensation."

"But you said you didn't want to get involved."

The attraction was so powerful it made his balls rattle, he told her. It was a miracle he'd gotten through the morning. Never before smitten – smite! what a perfect word for this assault of feeling – friends who had succumbed told him control hibernated like a fat old brown bear.

"The thing is," Livia said, "I can't tell if you want in or out."

"Out!" The word made a brash anguished sound like the bay of a sled dog at the lambent moonlight, but inside the Father's terror gaped into a vacuum of will. Somewhere in his core, Gino hadn't decided.

"Go away," Livia said. "Go out in the bush."

Driving south on the two-lane highway, empty of traffic except for an occasional truck, toward the head of the Stewart River, Gino's elation at escaping from terrible danger mounted. Soon, he'd be hurtling full throttle down the frozen Stewart River, his mind flying through the endless white wilderness. Oh, he'd be glad to be free of the shackles of priesthood for a week or ten days, glad to be away from the roil of human emotions people always expected their priest to lift.

At the trailhead, a plywood sled on runners, porting an aluminum tool box, waited for him, as Luc had promised. Strangely, Luc's four-wheeler was parked there as well. It was March and still cold, months before thaw would open the rivers that confluenced at Dawson, the Yukon and the Klondike, but the Stewart was shallow; breakup earlier. Gino rolled his gleaming black snow machine off the truck, roared the engine to life, and wove through a snarl of brush and trees to the riverbank. He thwacked the ice two, three times in different places with his ice axe. At least four inches, he guessed: completely safe.

Luc and Sally Archambault lived about forty miles up the Stewart River, in the near bush. Gino had loaded up with perishables he knew would be in short supply: lettuce, carrots, onions, any of the small shriveled vegetables and fruits of the North he could lay his hands on, along with fresh dairy products and a supply of good Irish whiskey and ale; he stashed it all along with his gear in the spacious metal container on the supply toboggan he now hitched to his machine. Pulling his hood over his tuque, a gush of relief and exhilaration raced through him. He remounted his snowmobile, a lean mean fast machine, the Harley of the North he secretly believed. In minutes, he was out on the ice, the wind chilling the temperatures well below zero on the flat open prairie of gelid river. Switching the handle warmers onto low, he zagged along a scar of rough ice through the frozen mantle of unbroken snow, a crust of white granite, crevassed and bumpy and harsh. Throttling up the engine faster, his flesh hummed in the rhythms of freedom, his spirit winging through the skies like an angel in training, aloft as only being alone in the bush could evoke. Everything was simple in the bush, life pared to basics, God close, or superfluous, as Luc would argue. Soon there was no trail at all, just the black machine and the white river, the brilliant sapphire sky, the green peaks of spruce on the banks, the yellow patina of sunlight.

The Archambault house stood alone on a sundrenched bluff in a grove of trees overlooking the river, its cold dignified beauty like an Alpine chalet. Though the temperature was still below freezing, Sally was outside in a sweater, enjoying the brilliant spring sun. So uncomplicated, Gino thought, the ride and his narrow escape from the love test keeping his mood buoyant. To the grind of living, the Archambaults brought grace. Luc trapped, skinned, fished, hunted, painted; Sally helped with the trapline, gardened, cooked, wrote; they home-schooled the kids, kept a dog yard; all of them were handy, tech-savvy and content with their lives.

Luc Archambault was a bourgeois French Canadian boy who'd run off to the bush on a lark and stayed because he loved the life. Medium-sized, muscular, bald on the pate, a yarn-spinner and a party boy as well as a talented artist, a good Catholic, in spite of his atheistic talk, Luc was as close to a friend as Gino had outside his seminary classmates. As darkness gathered, early because it was still the cusp of winter, Gino, Luc, Sally and their two kids sat down to a festive meal of moose tenderloin and the trimmings. When they got to coffee and whiskey, Luc's guffaw bounced around the log walls: he was expecting a friend from back home; he hoped Gino didn't mind sharing the guest quarters, as if these were more than a corner of the living room and an outhouse with two side by side holes on a slab of wood that everyone tromped across the snow to use. Gino shrugged, there was nothing he could do if he did mind. "Ah, that's why the ATV," he exclaimed.

"For the cheechako."

"New to the bush?" This was a surprise. Normally, Luc would escort newcomers in himself, not trust them with his favorite machine.

"To *this* bush," Luc replied. "Better than I am at some things."

Sally gave her breathy laugh. "Most things, *chéri*."

The next day was glorious: a sunrise dogsled ride, Gino's bony butt slamming up and down in the Cordura sled bag as twelve raring dogs, bootied and harnessed, sinuated through a winding trail, heedless of tree roots and ice clefts and spiky little rocks that shouldered through the snow blanket, hellbent on getting down to the river to run fast as a tempest. The wheel dog, hindmost on the gangline, the ballast of the team, lifted his leg to piss on the run and a flurry of yellow drops sluiced backwards and sideways, frozen into hail by the time they hit Gino. The lead dog had a head on her, that mad look in her eye every musher yammered on about; crazed like a winner, Luc had said, though he hadn't yet run her enough to know if she had sense too.

"Gee!" Luc hollered, and the dog, Riddles, veered to the right just a little late, the overshot causing the toboggan to zoom forward in its old trajectory, almost ejecting Gino like a rock from a slingshot.

"Not too good with the Gee-haws yet," Luc called, laughing.

But out on the river, in the vast envelope of silence broken only by the shush-shush of runners, Gino felt a rush of peace, a sense of life lived as it was meant to be. All twelve dogs stretched out before him, pounding *now now now now* as though there were nothing but the evermoving now, one second then the next then the next, the forward motion of a linear universe beating out its rhythm. A flock of snow buntings darted from a rocky outcrop on the riverbank in a swirl of motion that made the wind visible. A jay gave its raucous call and it sounded like laughter. I'm ready, Gino shouted, for Luc had promised he'd let Gino drive the team if he wanted.

During their stop, three of the dogs started to snarl and snap, but Luc pulled them apart before an impossible tangle of dogs resulted. After snacking the dogs, it was Gino's turn to drive. He yanked out the snow hook and mounted the runners, gesturing Luc to sit in the sled bag. Standing at the tip of the runners, clutching the handle-bow in front of him, a thrill of aliveness shivered through every neuron of his being. Time and again, he had proved himself in the North, hunting, climbing, hiking the Chilkoot, only to come home to the rectory and find he still thought of himself as a sissy, the boy from the foreign family, his face too gold in its hues, too Asian, his identifications too close to his mother. But dog driving! The steel of confidence poured through his bones. So this was what it meant to be an athlete, powerful in your body, focused in your mind, your heart, a muscle after all, strong enough to love even your enemies; so this was what God intended humans to be.

In the afternoon, Luc took him to an old sourdough's cabin, abandoned during the gold rush era and preserved by the winters. Low to the ground and mantled in white, it was a cramped little hovel, so squat that when Luc raised his head, it clanked against a ceiling beam. "*Tabernac,*" he muttered and laughed his hooting laugh. Set on a floor of bare hard ground, the bunk was made of plank and covered in ratty woolens, yet wide enough for two and, unbidden, up rose the image of the stranger in the fifth pew. Gino forced his gaze to the rickety table where a diary, its pages yellow and curled, lay open, and the first words seemed to mock him, *We have turned to each other, Hans and me, two ragged old prospectors, chilled by the endless night.* A yearning to steal the diary and get Livia to write about forsaken gay sourdoughs surged through him; here was a record, an actual historical artifact, that proved some of the tough old codgers who explored the North had been gay, like explorers throughout history, men who wanted to get as far away as possible from the constraints and shame societies laid on them. A miner's gear, including gold pans and buckets, was intact in the corner and he and Luc searched through it: one gold poke and Luc and his family would be set for life.

On their way back, the men were quiet, comfortable in their wordless camaraderie. Gino felt replete, strong, lusciously satisfied. Driving the dog team, he had unleashed a reserve of strength he didn't know he had. In quiet courage of the gay sourdoughs, he had felt an ancestry. He had beaten his own nature, surmounted the dangerous love test. As they eased their snowmachines around the last curves of trail to park, Gino noticed the four-wheeler was back in the yard.

Pronouncing it Onree, the French Canadian way, Luc performed the introduction. "Gino Laxa, Henry Brandon. Dr. Henry Brandon, Father Gino Laxa."

Color rushed up Gino's neck to splatter all over his hot, wind-reddened cheeks. This time he had no Good Book to hide behind.

"Destiny is having her joke with us," Henry Brandon said, mirth frolicking in his penetrating eyes. He looked as comfortable here as he had in church, his legs lanky in loose gray sweats.

"Appointment in Samarra," Gino muttered. A horrid story. Back in the days Iraq was Mesopotamia, a servant had traveled to the bazaar to shop for his master, a Baghdad merchant. Jostled, he turned to find Death, a woman in black, had singled him out. Racing home, he begged the merchant to lend him a horse and galloped off to Samarra. The merchant went down to the market to see if he could discover why the woman in black had threatened his servant. *I was startled to see him here in Baghdad*, Death replied, *for I have an appointment with him tonight in Samarra.*

"Ah, Somerset Maugham," the doctor said. "You came here to get away from me?"

"I like it out here."

"It seems we share sleeping quarters. I have a tent I can use, if you mind."

Gino gave a Samarran shrug, the abandonment of will to fate, kismet, God's omniscient hand.

After an evening of hearty drinking, tall tales, and a few hands of poker (won by the new Gino), when the Archambault family were lodged upstairs in their beds, urine jars on the floor by their sides, Gino and Henry made up their pallets side by side on the floor in the open space of the great room. Surrounded by windows, the moon pouring pale silvery light around the darkened isosceles of spruce, the stars a glittery dance against the infinite night, the intensity between them amplified. Henry reached out and the yearning was almost unbearable, but Gino drew on his new strength and turned away. *"C'est le destin,"* Henry whispered, before he rolled over to sleep, and the certainty of his utterance entered Gino's dreams. He was a kite, aloft, Henry far below, cradling the cable-thick string, guiding the kite towards the caress of the sun, stoking it with gusts of wind. Gino flew! He flew. Then he was adrift alone in the sky. Gone was his cross, his ring, the accoutrements of his office. Gone were his vestments. The sky was starless and thick with clouds, their cold moisture chilling his naked skin. Above him flew the Storch of the Bishop, a Vatican logo painted on the tail, a cross on each wing. Beside it flew a hooded figure in black, just arrived from the desert city of Samarra.

His long underwear soft against his skin, Gino slipped out the front so the twenty-some dogs in the back wouldn't howl their long weird moon-cries. An eerie light from a gibbous moon and the clutter of stars steeped the dark night. Beauty enveloped him, and in the far corner of the sky, the green flare of the aurora borealis started to shimmer. In wisps and rivers, thin gauzy light spilled across the sky, frothing into green peaks, ebbing, flaring in another corner, weaving and braiding into lacy patterns. The ethereal beauty eased the night into something friendly, soothing the terror evoked by the dream, its lonely arc emblematic of his life as a priest. God is near, Gino felt and thought about praying, too rare an impulse since Zeke's death.

A soft sound like a breeze susurrated beside Gino and he turned. Ringed by auroral light, Henry stood beside him, moccasins hugging his ungainly feet. He beared out his arms and Gino stepped in. Henry's mouth tasted of spice and moose, which seeped into the scents of whiskey and the church that lingered in his own. Henry steered a gentle course back to their pallets.

What a union they had, the two of them so sure of their passion, so unlike his boys of summer, Gino thought later, his mind still trying to process the shock of new feelings, the fierce yet delicate passion, the vivid sense of Henry's presence that made him hyperaware even as wild desire seared through him. By the end of the night they'd tried just about everything, laughing when something got clumsy or floppy, their camaraderie deepening. "So do you think they heard," he muttered as shafts of sunrise filtered through the trees and tinted the room in bright cherry colors.

"I think they'll smell us." Henry wrinkled his long flat nose. The stench of semen and sweat was everywhere.

Gino laughed because he didn't care. Luc knew anyway, so the whole family probably did. Still, another aroma wouldn't hurt, and he got up to make coffee.

Sally clumped down the stairs. She was in an old stained robe over flannel pajamas, fleece slippers so thick they looked like clown shoes, and her eyes were squinty from night discharge. "Not too awake without coffee," she muttered, pouring herself a cup, which she drank while she threw more logs into the wood stove and more scraps into a tall stockpot of slop for the dogs. "You have a good night?"

Gino felt radiance pour out of him, and saw a look cross her face that held a shadow of horror before she covered it with an awkward laugh.

"We gotta go," Gino said to Henry, when he went back to roll up their pallets. Henry was reading a book about the hippie-adventurers who'd settled the bush along the Stewart River and he grunted a sound of pleasure. A tour of Luc's trapline, they agreed would be perfect. It was near the end of the season, but the tents, big sturdy wall tents as comfortable as cabins, pitched at working intervals along the line, would still be stocked for winter use, so they'd only need to pack in clothes and emergency gear.

Luc had a locker full of game, mostly lynx and marten, to skin and prepare for market, and after breakfast, when they told him they were taking off for a few days, he wished them godspeed in a way that made Gino wonder if he'd set the whole thing up. Just an old romantic, Luc was, guided by an inner compass of love and instinct that Gino sometimes envied. In this case, he'd been right. Bliss followed Gino and Henry along the trails upriver as they entwined their sleeping bags in each wall tent on the trap line, and it found them again hunting for spring game along the banks of the Stewart, hiking and snowshoeing, ice fishing and downing pan-fried catch from their ungloved hands, juices running; discovering their shared love of the bush, of the North, of God, of whiskey, of every cranny and pore of each other's sweet naked flesh, of every bite and parry of each other's sharp agile minds. On the double plank bed in the old sourdoughs' cabin, they read aloud to each other from the journal of their ancestors. *We don't know why it took so long for us to find each other,* the old sourdough had written, *but it doesn't matter for love is the Yukon gold that we discovered. Tonight we ate the last of the potatoes, fried crispy in bear grease. We have nothing left but flour and grains and are on the last cord of logs for the fire. The winter temperatures have been forty below and colder for nearly two months and neither of us has the strength to weather another storm so violent we can't hunt or trap. But if I starve to death here with Hans, I will die contented. I have had my feast.* They did find gold, it turned out, and abandoned the cabin and the journal without recording their plans. "Hans," Gino murmured to Henry, struck by the concordance of initials. At night, he felt cradled by many arms, Henry's and history's, and he could hear echoes of the sourdoughs' hearts beating as he leaned into Henry's chest, swathed by the rangy body around him like a crescent, curving above his head and beneath his feet, protecting him completely, and Gino realized he had not spent a night with another soul in the twenty-two years since his ordination.

Since Gino had arrived, daytime had lengthened by 42 minutes, six minutes a day, a full half hour just in their days together in the bush, as though their union invoked sunlight and radiance. The day before Gino was due to leave, the sunlight shining warm as the first days of summer, the landscape mantled in winter snow, they sat on a skookum bench in a clearing and had The Talk.

"We can't be Out in Dawson," Gino said, the words catching low in his throat.

Sharp with awareness, Henry's eyes rested on him. "We can't hide, Gino."

Gino said what he swore he'd never say. "I want to leave the priesthood. I want to be with you."

The deep woods drew Henry's gaze, but it felt as though his eyes still shafted through Gino. "Did you want to leave the priesthood before you met me?"

It had been the last thing Gino wanted: being a priest fulfilled a yearning to matter in the world. "But this is different. I've never felt this way and I'm not going to give it up. Not for anything."

Henry's gaze roamed around the landscape, taking in, it seemed to Gino, the intense sapphire of the sky, the tiny new buds on the rosehips, the bright trilling warble of the snow buntings, the vast spruce forest that seemed to roll on forever. "A cup of tea," Henry said, the words sliding slowly out, "like the dried rosehip and chamomile we drank last night. It seemed honeycombed with flavors, so delicate, like nectar. Why do you think the food out here is so good? I mean it's just meat and potatoes, bread, vegetables. But it's saturated with the love that the Archambaults have for each other and for the bush." Henry looked back at the buds. "That's the thing; nature has seasons. Once you plant something, you have to know when to harvest it."

Gino felt a pain in his chest, a choke that came and went, leaving sadness he didn't understand. He didn't want to be defrocked, even by choice, even for something as crucial as this. He said as much to Henry.

Julie Brickman

Henry gave a whoop. "Castrated." His palm cupped his forehead as though rallying his thoughts. "*Crisse.* They take your testicles and hogtie them to the church – that's what celibacy does, it yokes you by the sacs of your manhood to the church, so when they cut you loose, they get to keep your balls. It's brilliant in a way. Machiavellian, but brilliant."

Why the Church, especially the big boys in the Vatican, were so rigid about the vow of celibacy had confounded Gino all his life. After all, seven popes in the first five centuries had been the sons of priests, and married bishops had been numerous. As a friend of his in Rome had reminded him, when he'd blessed an inn remodeled from a brothel, Cardinal Danielou was probably not the highest-ranking church official who had died in a whorehouse. "Holy crap," was all he said.

"Surely you've got some leeway. The Bishop has affairs and comes up to Dawson to gamble and drink, you said."

Zeke's story spilled out. Gino had never touched his foster son, in fact, had carefully protected him from any exposure to his rogue passions, but when Zeke was thirteen, he'd confessed to Gino that he had dreams about boys, not girls; that he was gay and wanted Gino to induct him, like the Man/Boy website recommended. Of course Gino had steadfastly refused, but one night, one horrible night, when Zeke and some friends were camping up the road to the Arctic, Gino brought a lover home, a college kid from Montana, who'd been juiced by the sweet lure of the forbidden. That night, around two or three in the morning, with no call or forewarning,

180

Zeke arrived home and caught them *in flagrante* in the bedroom.

Gino scanned Henry for narrowed eyes or a pinch of the forehead, but Henry's face was the hue of winter, the eyes sad and anguished, a mirror of Gino's unspoken interior.

"Zeke let out a scream so horrible, I thought something had happened to him, but then he leapt onto the bed and began punching my poor little hick. When he grabbed the pewter lamp I keep by my bedside, I snapped out of my shock and held him down while Montana snatched up his clothes and split. Zeke thrashed around in my arms, cursing and sobbing, and the next day, after we talked, the boy got out of town, with a bit of my money to expedite things, I might add. I promised Zeke it would not happen again, but it didn't help. He smashed up my things, cut up my clothing, even my vestments. You have to love *me, me!* he'd mutter, you have to be *my* lover.

"The irony of it! There I was, so proud of myself for sticking to my personal vow to stay away from anyone underage or local and then this. He had me by the gorge, I tell you. Because he said he would tell everyone I'd abused him if I didn't do what he wanted. The one gorgeous boy I stayed away from and look what happened."

Henry's large hand, cool from the biting air, traced patterns along Gino's wrist and hand. "How did the Bishop find out?" he asked.

"I don't think he did. Not for sure." Gino had told one or two people: his closest friend from his seminary days; the curator of Dawson's small museum; the writer Livia. "Anyhow, it leaked, the rumors."

"I'll bet. All those brothers and priests accused or convicted of abuse. The big Christian Brothers scandal. Not good timing."

Gino told Henry about finding Zeke, his face all bloated and purple, contorted in terror. "Which made me sure he hadn't intended to die, but meant for me to find him and save him. He thought we had some kind of mystical connection, that I would just know what he was doing, wherever I was. He'd clothed himself in a chasuble and stole he knew were my favorites and puked all over them." Gino felt a familiar nausea spasm through him, but when he gagged, he saw a film of moisture coat Henry's eyes and it calmed him.

"I keep imagining everything I didn't see. The walk from the rectory to the church doors, down the aisle in the center of the nave, to the sacristy. Did he kneel in the chancel? Did he pray? I know he thumbed through the vestments to find the ones he wore, so fouled by waste, so incredibly fetid and gastric, but did he try on others? I think about that every time I put one on. Zeke loved to costume, not in a tranny way, though he liked makeup, but as a way to unlock secrets, get the dope on people who confused or scared him. So he'd wear a big spade beard or old prospector duds. He liked to change identities, he told me, because he didn't have any of his own except" – Gino cringed – "as my boy. And what about all the planning he had to do? Buying the rope, testing its strength? Finding a hook strong enough, nailing it up to a beam? I bet he wanted a cross, but couldn't figure out how to attach himself to it; he nailed one above the hook, you know. I picture that too. Oh God. It hasn't felt right, praying since then. You see . . ." Gino turned, his blue-gray sloping eyes asking for mercy, expecting contempt. "I do want to leave the priesthood. My insides are tainted. I hate, Henry. I hate everyone some days."

Henry said nothing, but the gloss of his eyes reflected the trees that were mirrored in them and they seemed omni-empathic.

"He made one suicide attempt before the last one, so I should have seen it coming. But I didn't believe it. Even when he said to me, I'm going to kill myself if you don't love me, I didn't believe it. You don't you just don't." Gino choked on the surge of memory and guilt.

"Think of me as the person who loved you more than life. That's what Zeke wrote."

"But the legacy he left you is one of malice."

Henry's sinewy arms wrapped themselves around Gino's head and the pain lifted.

"It's been so lonely, " Gino whispered. "You have no idea. Being a priest is so lonely.

But you always have God. And then I didn't."

Back in Dawson, they separated, Henry to his spare rental bungalow, Gino back in the rectory. The tangled social circles of Dawsonites brought them together often, Henry a quiet counterpart to Gino's chatty conviviality. Romantically, they met in secret, deep in the nights. Henry snowshoed or trod silently across town to the rectory, leaving in the dark of the early morning, earlier as the solstice drew near. During June, Henry built himself a cabin across the river in West Dawson, the near bush where he could live in the solitude he loved. A one room A-frame with wrap-around lofts, the cabin had no plumbing, no electricity, no amenities at all except a wood stove, hand-built furnishings, outhouse, sauna, shower rig, generator. There they spent days together, Gino dissembling that he was on a trip or a conference, Henry accessible for medical emergencies by sat cell and beeper. In front of the stove that constituted Henry's kitchen, Gino boomed arias from his operatic repertoire, his feet tapping and bouncing, his body asway. He had not known this kind of happiness, he told Henry, and it made his insides serene and kept a blaze in his gut that inspired courage not fear. He thrived in their double life, because he didn't want to give up either of his loves, didn't see the crash coming except some nights in Henry's eyes.

Gino's sermons grew rich with love, his parish crowding as his reputation spread, drawing in errant Christians from all faiths. Long lines formed for the Eucharist and at the confessional for Father Gino suddenly seemed to know what to say to ease a person's suffering. Henry became known as a practitioner who blended western and native lore, peerless in both diagnosis and treatment, attracting people from all over the Territory, though he distanced himself from the accolades. "It makes me feel hollow," he told Gino, who basked in his own renown.

As the fall came and went, Gino saw the Bishop several times passing through Dawson or down in Whitehorse. In late February, when the Trek Over the

Top snowmachiners made their annual Dawson stop and Diamond Tooth Gertie's opened for a night of gambling and chorus line dancing, Gino brought Henry and the Bishop together. The three of them gambled together, delighting in the haven of an historical gambling site run by the town council, playing blackjack and poker, swilling microbrew and a few whiskeys. While Henry crossed the ice bridge to his West Dawson cabin, back at the rectory, over cognac and cheese, the Bishop asked what Gino planned to do.

"Do?"

"About you and Henry. You're obviously in love."

Gino flopped back in his wing chair, the swirl of the cognac in its snifter looking like a small whirlpool of agitation.

The Bishop told him about his own unforgettable years with an intelligent, beautiful woman he had loved.

"What did you do?"

"I'm here," he said, simply. "But others have left. It's really up to you. To this day, I don't know if I made the right choice."

"Rent-a-Priest," Gino muttered. It was a joke between them: if either one of them got in trouble for roaming, he could always join the organization of married and lapsed priests, continue to make a living as an ordained Catholic.

The organization, Celibacy is the Issue, had grown out of the escalating Catholic movement for legitimizing a tier of ordination for sexually active priests. "Visit God's Yellow Pages (Priests' Directory)," their website read, "or click your State below to locate a Married Catholic Priest near you."

185

"Don't you need proof?" Gino said softly, a challenge, though he knew suspicion was enough for the Vatican to authorize a transfer or a long stay in a retreat house.

Murmuring apologies, the Bishop riffled through the briefcase he'd left beside the rocker where he always sat. He handed Gino an envelope, and Gino recognized the parish logo in the upper left hand corner, his own stationary. Beneath it, he could see the still-childish scrawl of Zeke.

"He accuses you of sexual abuse."

"But it isn't true!" Gino, who had been a sexual adventurer his entire ordained life, was aghast.

"It won't matter." The Bishop's voice sounded gentle as a lover's whisper. "His death will be proof enough."

"May I have this?"

A complicity to overlook what they knew to be human folly existed among many in the Catholic hierarchy as long as it didn't interfere with the sacred duties of office, and Gino knew the Bishop understood what he meant. If the Bishop hadn't done anything with the letter by now, clearly he didn't want to.

"It's been two years," The Bishop said. "And I think about it every day. I know it by heart, every word."

With the Bishop watching, Gino studied the postmark, one day before Zeke had hanged himself, then read the contents of the letter. None of it was new to him, but he felt as if he were seeing it through the eyes of an outsider, and it was damning. *My name is Zeke. I am thirteen years old and I have been living with Father Gino Laxa in Dawson since my parents died four years ago in a crash with a moose on the highway. Father Gino saved me from a terrible life with foster parents who beat me and the other boys and then he saved me again when I almost went to the boys' jail in Whitehorse. But he does bad things to me. At night he comes into my room and he puts his hands on me and then makes me do him in my mouth or let him do me back there. If someone doesn't help me soon, I will die. Respectfully yours, Zeke Laxa.*

"You aren't going to use this." The paper twitched in Gino's hands. "You know it's a fabrication. You've kept it for two years."

"Does it matter if this one is a lie? What about all those other innocent boys? Doesn't this represent a truth about you?" The Bishop tucked the letter back in his briefcase, rolling the numerical lock until its clasp gave a metallic click

"I've never been with a single boy who didn't consent."

The Bishop sat quietly, his leathery face tired and far away. Through the branches of the tree outside, moonlight cast long shadows that quivered in a stir of north wind. Gino thought about Henry and warmth spread through him, the comfort of so many nights when the yaw of loneliness visited someone else's bed.

"I have a son," the Bishop said.

Attention sizzled up Gino's spine before his mind processed the news enough to mumble a question.

"My friend was pregnant when we stopped seeing each other. Nineteen years ago. It's why we broke up."

"So that makes you identify with Zeke?"

"With your boys of summer. Don't you see? My son could be one of them."

When they were together two days later, Gino told Henry about his conversation with the Bishop, how in his devastation, all he could think of was Henry. "I want to live with you," he said. "I've made up my mind to leave the priesthood."

Henry shook his head in his slow, thoughtful way. "It won't work."

"Of course it will! This is what we want, what you've pressured me for all these months."

"No, it's not." Henry's voice had an excess of calm that frightened Gino.

"What, then? Why the sudden change?"

The dark eyes went into luminous stillness, the finality in them worse than watching the letter slide back into the Bishop's briefcase.

"Gino, don't you see what's happened? Love has changed both of us, pushing us deeper into who we really are. I've become more and more solitary because all I need is a home in the bush, my work, and you. You've become more outgoing, ministering to people all over the Territory – the West even – developing relationships with everyone, no matter what faith, even agnostics and atheists. You thrive on it, Gino. You love being a priest. I think if the Bishop knows you're genuinely sorry and really are going to give up your boys, he won't do anything with the letter."

In June, months after Henry had left to take a post in the High Arctic, in the third pew in St. Mary's Catholic Church sat a beautiful college boy who prayed with excessive reverence, making himself obvious and seductive. Gino waited for the rush of desire to hit him and sure enough, a surge nearly felled him, a wash of intensity that hit his knees, his legs, his shaking hands, but the feeling behind it was not what he expected. Not desire, not urgency or yearning, no, what socked him so hard he almost toppled was rage. A fury so hot it seared his consciousness until the words he uttered boiled in the air.

His mind bifurcated, one part delivering his homily, the other on a frantic search. He felt enraged, wanted to pulverize the naïve allure from the fresh young face. It was Henry, he wanted. Henry! Not some sack of malleable flesh and downy balls. He didn't want this boy. He hadn't wanted any of them. A vision of the strong, savvy boys he'd known in school who'd lacerated him with bullying contempt for his nerdiness, his weird slanty eyes, his sissy fairy ways, taunting him that he'd never have kids, had no chance at immortality, would lurk forever at the periphery of life, rocked through his memory. And the old chasm of fear opened up, the dread of loneliness so vast he'd go insane. Every boy he'd fucked in the ass or in the mouth struck at a tormentor. His seductions, then, were a form of rage? His charm, veiled cruelty? Yes, he thought, expectorating the word right into his sermon. But he would never risk it all again when he hadn't for Henry. It was over now, that brand of passion, over because Henry loved him, because he knew real love, would always know love.

When he got to the Eucharist, Father Eugenio Laxa cried. Love had flung open the door to the abyss of his interior and sorrow flowed out like Christ's blood. The only way out of loneliness was to join his life with Henry's. The only way into worth was to stay a priest. He was moored on the prongs of an insoluble dilemma. His yearning for Henry would always be there. His love of the priesthood would always be core.

Stepping down, Father Eugenio Laxa strode across the chancel down the short corridor through the side door and followed the back path to the rectory.

Acknowledgements

A few of my close friends read and critiqued some of the stories in this collection, encouraging me in ways too deep and vast to enumerate; to them I give my deepest gratitude and love. For always believing in me, even during the worst of his suffering, I thank my late husband, Bob Hoyk. For her transcendent friendship and unwavering belief in me as a writer, I thank Sena Jeter Naslund. For a friendship without which I could not have survived the hard times and her brilliant writer's mind, I thank Deidre Woollard. For his support and incredible insight as a reader, I thank Philip Deaver. For his ability to map and discuss the path of the creative life, I thank Daniel Koulack. For his inimitable friendship, unique mind, and the flurries of email that pulled me out of many wee hours of despond, I thank Christopher Klim. For close reading and exquisite writerly friendships, I thank Rhoda Green, Katy Yocom, Maryann Lesert and Pam Sexton.

Friends and colleagues have supported my writing in an astonishing range of ways. For hospitality and guidance in the United Arab Emirates, I thank Fatma al-Sayegh and Linda C. MacConnell; for his deep desert tour I thank Fouad Hani Saimoua. For expert vetting of Arabian Gulf content, I thank Dr. Joseph A. Kechichian. For hospitality and guidance in the Yukon Territory, I thank Paula Pasquali, Kathryn, Kyla and Rock Boivin. For granting me a position as writer-in-residence in the Yukon Territory, I thank the Yukon Arts Council and the

Berton House Writers Retreat. For warm friendship and a creative venue to write in, I thank Karen Ziccardi; also David Gilbert. For invaluable support of my writing in diverse ways, I thank Arthur Salm, Carolyn Jenks, Bret Lott, the late Marcia Woodruff Dalton, Dave Heuck, Jenny Heuck, Sarah Jo Sinclair, Linda Busby Parker, Charlotte Rains Dixon, Karen Redding, Ed Kaufman, Nina Brickman, Susan Vreeland, Murzban Schroff, Susan Dalsimer, Pat Gifford, Audrey and Phillip Unger.

I also want to thank the remarkable people at Spalding University's brief-residency MFA in Writing Program, where I am lucky enough to teach and mentor, who have created an ambiance extraordinaire to succor the creative life and evoke the best from a writer. This program and its fabulous faculty, staff and students have inspired me to aim for freshness and excellence over the years; without them these stories would not exist. My deepest thanks go to Director Sena Jeter Naslund, whose extraordinary vision and genius created and sustains the program; Administrative Director, Karen Mann, whose dexterous mind mounts its astonishing range of offerings; Associate Director Kathleen Driskell who solves anything with a wink and a laugh; Administrative Assistants Katy Yocom and Gayle Hanratty who give so generously of their talents; colleagues from the original faculty Robin Lippincott, Melissa Pritchard, Greg Pape, Dianne Aprile, Roy Hoffman, Luke Wallin, Ellie Bryant; and from the later faculty: Philip F. Deaver, Richard Goodman, Susan Campbell Bartoletti, Mary Yukari Waters, John Pipkin, Kirby Gann, Neela Vaswani, Wesley Brown, Eleanor Morse, Jody Lisberger, Debra Kang Dean, Molly Peacock, Bob Finch, Joyce MacDonald, Elaine Orr, who have given me praise, advice, encouragement, ideas and inspiration over the years.

I also want to thank the students whose close work with me has enriched my writing life, especially those who have participated in the book-length manuscript workshops, the pioneer group: Deidre Woollard, Maryann Lesert, Katy Yocom, Charlotte Rains Dixon, Linda Busy Parker; and later groups: Karen Mann, Lynda Archer, Leesteffy Jenkins, Deborah Miller and Jim Robertson; Jim Wayne, Tay Berryhill, Catt Foy, Mary Knight and Adriena Dame; those who have worked frequently or in extended ways with me: Katy Yocom, Jim Robertson, Kate Beer, LaEsha Sanders, Lora Hilty, Kay Gill, Vanessa Gonzales; those who have acknowledged me in celebrating their own publications: Maryann Lesert, Linda Busby Parker, Jackie Gorman, Andrew Beahrs, Lucrecia Guerrero, Cory Jackson. My thanks also goes to many wonderful writers, whom I don't have space to name, who have chosen to work with me as a mentor or in workshops. You are all part of this book.

Everlasting thanks goes to my family: my late parents, Molly & Leo Brickman, who nurtured the first blooms of creativity and intelligence in me, as did my late brother, Philip Brickman, and to my aunt, Beatty Zack, who continues to do so.

Profound thanks is also due to the superb creative team that made this book happen: editor, Christopher Klim of Hopewell Publications; photographers, Karen Redding and Dennis Jones; cover artist, Jonathan Weinert; social media consultant, Deidre Woollard.

CPSIA information can be obtained at www.ICGtesting.com
Printed in the USA
BVOW08s0958100913

330785BV00001B/1/P